Hemlock for the Holidays
A FINE ART MYSTERY

Books by Paula Darnell

DIY Diva Mystery Series

Death by Association

Death by Design

Death by Proxy

A Fine Art Mystery Series

Artistic License to Kill

Vanished into Plein Air

Hemlock for the Holidays

Historical Mystery

The Six-Week Solution

Hemlock for the Holidays
A Fine Art Mystery

PAULA DARNELL

CR
Campbell and Rogers Press
Las Vegas

CR

Campbell and Rogers Press

This is a work of fiction. Characters, names, events, places, incidents, business establishments, and organizations portrayed in this novel are the product of the author's imagination or are used fictitiously.

Library of Congress Control Number: 2021905821
ISBN: 9781887402231

Publisher's Cataloging-in-Publication Data
provided by Five Rainbows Cataloging Services

Names: Darnell, Paula Jean, author.
Title: Hemlock for the holidays / Paula Darnell.
Description: First edition. | Las Vegas : Campbell and Rogers Press, [2021] | Series: [A fine art mystery] ; [3]
Identifiers: ISBN 9781887402231 (paperback) | ISBN 9781887402255 (ePub)
Subjects: LCSH: Women artists—Arizona—Fiction. | Craft festivals—Arizona—Fiction. | Poisoning—Arizona—Fiction. | Murder—Investigation—Arizona—Fiction. | LCGFT: Cozy mysteries.
Classification: LCC PS3604.A7478 H46 2021 (print) | LCC PS3604.A7478 (ebook) | DDC 813/.6—dc23

Cover design by Nicole Hutton of Cover Shot Creations
Formatting by Polgarus Studio

First Edition

Published by Campbell and Rogers Press
www.campbellandrogerspress.com

Dedicated, with appreciation,
to artists and art lovers everywhere

Chapter 1

"Santa! Over here!" Belle called, as she waved to jolly Mr. Claus, who stood atop the passing float, surrounded by elves busily depositing toys in his sleigh.

"Ho! Ho! Ho!" he exclaimed, as he blew her a kiss.

The jolly red-suited gent, none other than my bestie's husband Dennis, had been drafted to play Santa in Lonesome Valley's annual Christmas parade when the original actor had come down with a case of food poisoning just a few hours before the parade was scheduled to begin.

"He's really into his role," I said, as the giant float slowly progressed down Main Street. "How did you plump him up? He actually looks kind of roly-poly."

"I wrapped him with fluffy batting before he put on the costume. I think it's working pretty well."

"For sure. He's a big hit."

Santa's float was followed by another featuring a giant, twinkling Christmas tree surrounded by beautifully wrapped presents. Children of members of Lonesome Valley's Downtown Merchants' Association sat among the gifts, waving shyly to the crowds that lined both sides of Main Street.

"Oh, look! Here come the carolers." Belle pointed to the next float, which was large enough to accommodate the Lonesome Valley Pioneers, who performed at many community events. We spotted Rebecca and Greg Winters, a couple Belle and I had met in the spring, when we were walking our dogs in the little park a few blocks from our houses.

The choir began its rendition of "The Twelve Days of Christmas" with Rebecca and Greg singing the first verse in duet. The only decoration on the choir's float was a small tree graced by a few pears and a lone partridge. Each time the choir sang the refrain "and a partridge in a pear tree," the singers all gestured toward the tree, and the partridge squawked, much to the delight of the spectators along the parade route.

"What a perfect day for the parade," I said. The Arizona sun shone in a cloudless, blue sky, and there wasn't so much as a breeze.

"Yes, it's great," Belle agreed. "Not like last year, when the wind gusted so much Santa lost his hat and Frosty blew over and fell right off the float. Of course, that happened before you moved here. I can't believe you've lived next door for—what is it?—just ten months now. It seems like we've been friends forever."

"Yes, it does," I said, putting my arm around her, "and I couldn't have better friends. If it weren't for you and Dennis, I might still be trying to adjust to my new life."

Instead, I felt perfectly at home in my tiny house with my amiable golden retriever Laddie and my mercurial calico cat Mona Lisa for company. I'd chosen the little house because it featured an attached art studio that was the same size as the house's living area. A year ago, I'd been trying to come to terms with my recent, unexpected divorce. My husband Ned had decided to drop that bomb on the same night as my one-and-only solo art show at the Crystal Star Gallery in Kansas City.

He'd announced that he planned to marry Candy, his office assistant, who's only a couple of years older than our daughter Emma. What he'd neglected to say was that Candy had a baby on the way. I'd been so excited preparing for my show that I hadn't had a clue!

Luckily, I'd snapped out of my panic mode after a few months to plan my new life. It wasn't long before I made the move from Kansas City to Lonesome Valley to pursue a career as a full-time artist, and I didn't regret it for a second.

Belle and I watched and cheered from the sidelines as several more floats passed by. A nineteenth-century stagecoach followed, pulled by four handsome horses, their manes and tails braided with red and green streamers. The sleigh bells hung around their necks jingled merrily as they pulled the coach along. The stage's driver sported traditional Western garb, with one exception. He'd substituted a plush red Santa hat for the Stetson he normally wore. His wife, decked out in a gorgeous, red velvet cape trimmed with white faux fur, rode beside him. Their three children peeped out the windows of the stagecoach and waved to the crowd. A high-profile couple, Melinda Gibbs was Lonesome Valley's mayor, and her husband Bob operated a large equestrian training center and horse stables at their ranch a few miles north of town.

Since the Gibbses never missed an opportunity to promote Lonesome Valley's galleries, all the artists at the Roadrunner, a cooperative art gallery where I displayed my oil paintings, appreciated their support.

Last up, the Lonesome Valley High School band marched past us, stepping smartly while they played "Rockin' Around the Christmas Tree." The crowd clapped enthusiastically, then began to disperse after the band passed by.

"I'm going to pick up a few gifts," Belle said. "Should I meet you at the Roadrunner in about an hour?"

"Perfect. Then we can see how Dennis is coming along with his Santa act." Dennis had agreed to play Santa for a group of preschoolers who'd have their pictures taken with him after the parade.

Belle crossed to the opposite side of Main Street, while I walked a block to the Roadrunner, curious to find out whether the parade-goers had stayed to shop. I hoped to improve my sales in December, especially since I'd had a bad month in November, and my finances were looking a bit tight, although I was in better shape than I'd been when I'd first moved to Lonesome Valley. The Roadrunner isn't the only place I sell my paintings, but it's my main venue. I also try to keep things going with studio tours, commissioned pet portraits, and even wholesale accounts with a few local boutiques, where I sell my abstract, dyed silk scarves.

With fingers figuratively crossed, I approached the Roadrunner and was pleased to see several people entering the gallery ahead of me.

Inside, a crush of people crowded around the jewelry counter and cash register, where Carrie and Ralph, two of our members, waited on customers. I was pleased that eighty-five-year-old Ralph kept pace as he handled the transactions. A few months earlier, his arthritis had plagued him so much that it had been difficult for him to move, but since his doctor had prescribed a different pain medication, he no longer relied on a cane.

Pamela, our gallery director, and my friend Susan, an awesome watercolorist who also sculpts huge animals in papier-mâché, were helping other customers as they browsed the paintings. I headed down the hallway and deposited my coat in our meeting room, then returned to the front of the gallery and stowed my purse in a drawer under the counter.

"Excuse me," a gray-haired woman carrying a large shopping bag said. "Do you work here?"

"Yes. How may I help you?"

"I saw a little painting of a cactus flower in the back."

"Let's take a closer look," I said, accompanying her around the divider to the back room.

She pointed to a group of cactus flowers. "I really like these," she said, "but I can't decide which one to buy."

"Do you have a place in mind to hang it?" I asked.

"Yes, I was thinking above a little table in my entryway. The walls are light beige, so I suppose any color would do—maybe the white flower?"

"How about the pink one? It could add a nice touch of color."

"I do like that one," she said, stepping in for a closer look. "Yes, I think you're right. I'll take it."

I carefully removed it from the wall and carried it to the front for her. There was a line at the register, so I jumped in to help Ralph, and we had soon checked out all the waiting customers.

"Enjoy it!" I said, waving at the woman I'd assisted as she left the gallery, carrying her painting.

Although Pamela was talking to a group of people near the door, the crowd had thinned, and I joined Susan.

"Amanda, I'm glad you came in when you did. It was getting crazy. I didn't think we'd be so busy after the festivities, but it looks as though things have calmed down now."

"Were you able to watch the parade?"

"We had a bird's-eye view from the balcony upstairs. It was

great. I thought the squawking partridge was so cute. Oh, look who's here!" A man wearing a jeans jacket entered the gallery.

I didn't recognize the newcomer, but Susan seemed pleased to see him when he approached and gave her a kiss on the cheek.

"Eric, I haven't seen you for ages!" Susan exclaimed after she'd introduced us.

"Yeah, I've been busy, too. Business is way down. I'm barely hanging on there, but things are about to take a turn for the better in a big way."

"That's good news."

"Yeah, I'm psyched. Timing couldn't be better. Anyway, I thought I'd pop in for a minute to say 'hi.' Figured you'd be here. Looks like you've been busy." He nodded at the large papier-mâché zebra that stood in the window. "As soon as I saw it, I knew it had to be yours. Say, do you have time to come by the house tomorrow evening? There's something I'd like to show you."

"I suppose I could stop by for a few minutes. Amanda and I were planning on going out to dinner tomorrow. Would you like to join us?"

"Well, all right, if it's OK with Amanda."

"Of course. The more, the merrier, and this is certainly the season to be merry," I agreed.

"All right. We're on. Text me the time and place, and I'll see you ladies tomorrow."

We watched him as he made his way to the door and stepped onto the sidewalk in front of the gallery.

"I hope he's right about things improving for him." Susan sighed. "About two years ago, his wife was killed in a terrible helicopter crash. She was my best friend."

"Susan, I'm so sorry. I didn't know."

"I don't talk about it much. It still hurts, and whenever I see Eric, it hurts even more. I haven't been avoiding him exactly, but I haven't gone out of my way to see him, either. I know he has financial problems now, too."

The gallery had almost cleared out by this time, and we joined Ralph and Carrie at the jewelry counter.

"Say, wasn't the guy you were just talking to the owner of Thrifty Buys?" Carrie asked.

"Yes. Eric Thompson," Susan confirmed.

"I heard the place is going under."

"I don't know about that," Susan said.

"It's true," Ralph interjected. "I saw the bankruptcy notice in the newspaper yesterday. He's filed for Chapter 7."

Chapter 2

"So I guess that means he's not going to try to reorganize," Susan said thoughtfully.

"It's a real shame," Carrie said. "No more Thrifty Buys. I always used to pick up a copy at the grocery store, but I suppose most classifieds are online now."

"I suppose." Susan frowned. "Eric must be having a worse time than I realized."

"But he said he anticipated a big change for the better," I reminded her.

"That's true," Susan agreed. "By the way, I apologize for not checking with you before I invited him to have dinner with us."

"It's totally fine. I'm looking forward to it. It's been a while since we had one of Miguel's margaritas."

"Would you mind if we went somewhere else instead? It's just that Miguel's was Natalie's favorite restaurant. She and Eric used to go there all the time."

"All right. You never mentioned to him where we planned to go, so we can change it to anywhere."

"Shall we try that new place out on the highway?"

"OK. See you there at six?"

After we settled on the time, I went to the meeting room to

collect my coat. Since Belle would arrive soon, I picked up my purse from the drawer by the register and went to the front to keep a lookout for her. When I saw her coming across the street, I waved goodbye to the gallery members and dashed outside.

"Do you think Santa's done with his photo shoot yet?" I asked.

"He should be getting close."

We walked to the parade's staging area nearby, in the courthouse's parking lot, where we found Santa and his elves posing for a picture with a little boy who kept pulling on Santa's beard. After his mom cajoled him into behaving, the photographer snapped his final picture of the day.

"All set, Santa?" Belle asked.

"Ho! Ho! Ho!" Dennis mugged for the little boy's benefit, before lowering his voice. "Let's go. I can't wait to get out of this costume. I need to ditch the beard, the wig, and the batting before I melt."

"You do look a bit uncomfortable," Belle noted. "Your face is all red, but you did a terrific job."

"Thank you, Mrs. Claus. Too bad there wasn't a costume for you. You could have ridden on the float, too."

"That's OK. I'm fine with being the support staff." Belle chuckled.

When Belle pulled into their garage, Dennis said a quick goodbye to me, before he rushed inside, eager to change out of his Santa costume.

"Have you decided which cookies to take to the cookie exchange at Rebecca's tomorrow?" Belle asked, as we got out of the car.

"I think I'm going to make pinwheels. I like them, but I never seem to think about making them except around the holidays. What about you?"

"I've already made mine, because I think bourbon balls are better after a day or two."

"We take two dozen, right?"

"Yes, and don't forget to bring enough copies of your recipe for everybody."

"Will do. See you tomorrow."

I ducked out of the garage and crossed Belle's front lawn to my carport, where I entered my house through the side door. Laddie had heard me coming and was waiting for me on the other side. He jumped up and down with glee at my arrival. My golden retriever much preferred my company to that of Mona Lisa, who usually either ignored or snubbed him, depending on her mood, although, occasionally, she felt friendly and curled up next to him for a cat nap.

Mona Lisa didn't make an appearance as I petted Laddie and gave him a hug. He followed me the few steps into the living room. "Mona Lisa, Mona Lisa," I sang to the tune of the song of the same name, popularized by Nat King Cole. Although my calico kitty didn't always respond to my latest ploy to tease her out of her hiding places, she came creeping down the hallway, approached me stealthily, and wound around my ankles, mewing as she rubbed against me. I picked her up for a cuddle, but she didn't tolerate it for long. She leapt down, found her feather toy in the corner, and dragged it to me. The message was clear: it was kitty playtime. I obliged her, flicking the feather back and forth while she chased it and pounced over and over. Laddie lay beside me, his eyes following her every move, but he didn't interfere or try to join the game. He'd learned long ago that he might be rewarded for his interest with a swat as she raked her sharp claws across his nose, so he kept a safe distance.

I rewarded Laddie's patience by playing catch with him in the backyard after I wrapped up the game with Mona Lisa. Like my persnickety calico kitty, Laddie never tired of playing, so I had to be the one to finally call a halt to fetching the ball.

By this time, it was late afternoon, and the light in the sky was fading fast. I preferred to work on my oil paintings during the day, when I had natural as well as artificial light in my studio. I decided to defer my cookie baking until morning. Since the dough had to chill once I'd made it, I could paint for a while after I refrigerated it, before I turned on the oven and started baking.

I was eager to finish my painting of Mr. Big, Belle's energetic little white dog and Laddie's pal. My Christmas gift to Belle and Dennis, the painting was nearing completion. Because I wanted it to be a surprise, I hid the canvas in a closet in my studio whenever I wasn't working on it. Belle often visited me, and I didn't want her to see it before we exchanged gifts.

It would be my first Christmas in my little house, and I felt lucky that my daughter Emma, my son Dustin, and my parents would all be coming for the holidays. I didn't have a guest room or, indeed, much spare room at all, but Emma, who planned to spend most of the break between semesters with me, had dibs on the hide-a-bed in the living room. Dustin and my parents would be staying next door, although their hosts wouldn't be there. Belle and Dennis planned a quick trip to Michigan to visit their children and grandchildren. Mr. Big always went with them when they drove, but, since they were flying this time, he'd stay behind with Laddie and me. The two dogs spent so much time together that I knew Mr. Big would feel right at home, although I had no doubt he'd miss Belle and Dennis.

I went to bed, thinking about my menus for Christmas Eve

and Christmas Day. Soon, I was dreaming of sugarplums and, before I knew it, Mona Lisa was pouncing on my head and Laddie was tapping my arm with his paw, urgently requesting me to get up. I rolled out of bed, and we began our morning routine. Once we'd had breakfast and I'd downed a couple of cups of strong tea, I mixed the dough for my pinwheel cookies and separated it, adding chocolate to half. Then, I covered the mixing bowls and set them inside the refrigerator. While the dough chilled, I made good progress on my portrait of Mr. Big. I figured I should easily be able to finish it in the next few days. I moved the canvas back into its hiding place in the closet before I rolled out the dough, sliced it, and baked the cookies. I kept a close eye on their progress after I put them into the oven so I could pull them out when they were at just the right degree of doneness.

I watched Mona Lisa's every move while I let the cookies cool, because she'd been known to jump up onto the counter, but she behaved herself, watching me from atop her kitty tree while Laddie stretched out at my feet. Once the cookies had cooled, I put the pinwheels into a red plastic container and set it in the back of my SUV. Rebecca's house was several blocks away, and, even though Belle and I could easily have walked, the thin-soled ballet flats she planned to wear weren't exactly walking shoes.

Rebecca had said to dress casually, so I put on a burgundy tunic over black leggings and added a gold chain necklace with crystals interspersed for a bit of holiday sparkle.

It seems as though every time I get ready to go out, I find another gray hair, which I always promptly pluck, and today proved no exception. Although my fiftieth birthday had passed a few months earlier, I still couldn't believe I'd logged five decades. It definitely was taking some getting used to.

I didn't want to dwell on the past. I had a whole new life unfolding with a new career, one I'd chosen for myself, new friends, and possibly a new man in my life. Brian had moved into the vacant house next door in September, and we were getting to know each other. Since his work on an oil rig in the Gulf of Mexico took him away from home for four-week chunks of time, and I was a bit hesitant about committing to a new relationship, we were taking it slow. He was away at work right at the moment and wouldn't be back in Lonesome Valley until after Christmas, but I was looking forward to our New Year's Eve date.

Laddie leaped up and bounded to the kitchen door, where he waited expectantly, his tail swishing back and forth rapidly. Belle's knock came a few seconds later. When he realized that Belle and I were about to depart, my golden retriever looked at me mournfully with his big brown eyes and whimpered softly.

"It's OK, Laddie," I assured him. "We'll be back later."

Reconciled to our departure, he lay down by the door, where he'd probably station himself until I returned. In the meantime, I knew he'd nap.

Outside, at my SUV, I asked, "Would you like to put your cookies in the back, Belle?"

"No need. I can hold them."

"OK, then; we're off."

It took only a few minutes to drive the short distance to Rebecca's home. We saw a couple other women at her door as I pulled into a spot by the little park across the street from the Winterses' house.

Inside, our hostess greeted us, and we joined the group gathered in the living room. Except for Rebecca, Belle and I didn't know the other women, but Rebecca made introductions all around, and we were soon becoming acquainted with three of Rebecca's neighbors and two members of the Lonesome Valley Pioneers.

"Ladies, we're going to save all our cookies for the exchange, so that everybody will have two dozen to take home. But that's no reason to deprive ourselves of holiday goodies, so I've set out a few snacks for us in the dining room." Rebecca slid open the pocket door that separated her living room and dining room, revealing a lovely decorated table laden with food.

"I have hot chocolate or coffee," she announced. "If anyone would prefer tea or a cold drink, just let me know."

"This looks wonderful, Rebecca," I said, and the other women chimed in.

We all stood up, but before we could move into the dining room, Skippy and Tucker, the Winterses' two wiggly terriers, rushed in and bounced around our feet. Fearing we might step on one of the lively little fellows, we froze in our tracks.

Chapter 3

"Sorry, honey," Greg said to Rebecca as he followed the dogs
in. "They got away from me. We'll be out of your way in a
minute. Come here, boys." Greg stooped to gather up the pups.
After he'd snapped on their leashes, he set them down and led
them toward the front door. I was sure they were headed across
the street to the park, where Belle and I had first met Greg when
we were all walking our dogs.

"They're so cute!" Mary, one of the choir members, said.

"They keep us on our toes; that's for sure," Rebecca
commented.

We drifted into the dining room and helped ourselves while
Rebecca served the hot chocolate and coffee. A nice cup of hot
chocolate sounded good to me. I sipped it and turned to
Rebecca to tell her how much I liked it.

"I'm glad Greg decided to take Skippy and Tucker to the
park. Maybe some fresh air will cheer him up a bit. He's been
in a terrible mood ever since he read the paper this morning."

"I must have missed something. I don't remember reading
any distressing news in this morning's paper."

"Oh, it wasn't the Sunday paper. Greg sometimes doesn't
read the news right away. The legal notice that upset him ran a

few days ago. Someone he loaned quite a bit of money to has filed for bankruptcy."

"You don't mean Eric Thompson, by any chance?"

"Yes, that's the guy. He's Greg's distant cousin."

"I just met him yesterday when he came into the gallery. My friend Susan told me Eric's wife was killed in a horrible helicopter crash a couple of years ago."

"Yes, it was awful. The pilot died, too. They were on one of those aerial tours of the Grand Canyon at the time, and Natalie was going to write a travel article about it. Greg told Eric not to worry about repaying the loan right away, but I know he expected to get our money back eventually. It doesn't look like that's going to happen now. Oh, well, what can you do?"

"You don't seem too upset about it."

Rebecca shrugged. "It's not as though we're hurting for money. Greg says it's the principle of the thing, but, in this case, it just seems better to let it go. I kind of figured the loan was going to end up a gift, because Eric may be a nice guy, but he's never been much of a businessman. Then, when he lost Natalie, he pretty much fell apart."

"Rebecca," one of the other women interrupted, "wherever did you find your cute Santa mugs? I'd love to get some. I know my grandkids would adore them."

"Oh, they're vintage, actually. I've had them forever, but you're welcome to borrow them for your holiday celebration if you like."

"You're sure you don't mind?"

"Not at all. We won't be home for Christmas this year, anyway. We're going to spend the holidays with the kids in Houston. Well, I guess it's about time to get this show on the road." She produced envelopes for us to put our recipes in and passed around the recipe cards that we'd all filled out.

"You should have eight recipes, counting your own," she told us. "We each brought two dozen cookies, so take three of each, and you'll have a nice variety. I set up everything on the kitchen counter. I have some extra plastic trays and wrap there, too, if you need them."

We all trooped into the kitchen and began putting our cookies into the containers we'd brought. Rebecca had placed little antique tongs beside each platter or tin of cookies, making it easy to transfer the cookies into our own containers. As I'd hoped, there were no duplicates. Besides the pinwheels I'd brought and Belle's bourbon balls, Rebecca and her other guests had all made enticing contributions.

"I never met a cookie I didn't like," Mary enthused.

I felt the same way. If my cookie collection stayed within my reach, I wouldn't have any left to share when my family visited.

"Uh, Belle, do you have room in your freezer for my cookies?" I asked. "I'm afraid they'll never make it to Christmas if I take them home with me."

"Sure, no problem. Since we're not going to be here for Christmas, I haven't stocked up."

"Oops, I almost forgot," Rebecca said, grabbing a large basket from the counter opposite the cookie display. "Please help yourself to some fudge." The basket was full of small red tins, each decorated with a felt snowman on top.

"How cute!" one of Rebecca's neighbors exclaimed. "Did you make the snowman?"

"Yes. I was in the craft store the other day, and the felt was calling my name, I guess."

"Are you going to decorate some of these for our booth at the craft fair Saturday?" Tammy, one of the choir members, asked. "We can charge more since the tin will be decorated."

"Well, I hadn't thought about it, but, sure, I can put some of the fudge in tins."

"Is that the Winter Craft Fair at the high school you're talking about?" Belle asked.

"Yes. The choir always sells candy and baked goods. It's one of our best fundraisers."

"I'm going to be there, too," Belle noted, "for the Library Auxiliary."

"Me, too," I chimed in. "The Roadrunner has a booth reserved in the gym."

"I always go to the high school fair," Carmen, one of Rebecca's neighbors, said. "I buy a lot of unique Christmas gifts there. I guess I'll see you all on Saturday. I should get going now. I promised to be home in time to help put the Christmas lights around our hedges."

For a moment, I felt a wave of painful emotion wash over me as I remembered Christmases past and decorating the house with Emma and Dustin. Ned, who hadn't normally taken much interest in family activities, would even climb a ladder to hang lights on the house. I let the memories fade and pulled myself back to reality. My family was different now, but they would be with me for Christmas, and I felt thankful we'd be together.

"Amanda, are you OK?" Belle looked at me with concern.

"Oh, sure. Just thinking. Every once in a while, the past comes back to haunt me."

Belle knew exactly what I meant. "Your first Christmas in Lonesome Valley is going to be wonderful, and I just know you'll have a happy new year, too!"

Chapter 4

Although we lingered for a while at Rebecca's, I had ample time before I needed to meet Susan and Eric for dinner. I took Laddie for his second walk of the day. Rebecca's neighbor wasn't alone in spending some time on a sunny weekend putting up Christmas decorations. Along our route, I saw several people hanging lights or setting up yard displays. Besides lights, the neighborhood was filled with Santas, reindeer, sleighs, snowmen, gingerbread houses, and nativity scenes.

My own Christmas decorating was minimal so far, due to the fact that all the holiday decorations Ned and I had accumulated during our twenty-five-year marriage were still in the house where we'd lived back in Kansas City, the same house my ex-husband now occupied with Candy and their baby. I hadn't taken much with me when I'd moved to Lonesome Valley—my clothes, art supplies, and just enough furniture and household goods to get by on.

Belle had made me a beautiful wreath studded with brightly colored Christmas tree ornaments, and I'd hung it on my front door immediately. Holiday decorations for inside proved more problematic since Mona Lisa showed far too much interest in anything bright or shiny she found on a tabletop, so, thus far,

I'd hung some Christmas cards on ribbons on the living room walls, and she'd shown no interest in those. I purchased a small artificial tree to put in the studio, and I had to remember to keep the door closed so that Mona Lisa wouldn't sneak in because she wanted to bat at the little tree's lights and bulbs in the worst way.

With a plaintive meow, Mona Lisa came running to me as soon as Laddie and I returned from our walk. I picked her up and held her, but she soon began to wiggle, and I set her down on the wide arm of my one-and-only living room chair. Dinnertime was fast approaching, and both my pets knew it. Their anticipation often started half an hour before the actual event. They kept a close eye on me while I checked my phone for messages. I'd missed a text from Susan, saying she'd see me soon, and another from Emma, with a picture of her dorm door, which she and her roommate had decorated for the holidays. She was busy studying for semester finals now, but as soon as she took her last exam, she'd be on a flight to Phoenix, and I'd pick her up at Sky Harbor Airport. I quickly responded to both texts before I put my cell phone in my bag. I left lights on in the living room and kitchen so that I wouldn't be coming home to a dark house.

His tummy full, Laddie was ready for his evening nap, and he took my departure in stride this time.

Susan and I had heard good things about the new restaurant on the outskirts of town, so I hadn't minded when she'd suggested it, instead of Miguel's. Although I couldn't remember the name of the place, I knew exactly where it was. When I arrived, it looked busy. A group of people were standing around outside the front door. I didn't see Susan among them, but I spotted her blue Honda in a corner of the parking lot and found a spot nearby. As I emerged from my car, I noticed Eric getting out of a small pickup truck that had a missing tailgate. I waved to him, but he didn't notice. As he walked toward the restaurant, a man standing near the restaurant went over to him.

They both stopped in the middle of the parking lot, but I couldn't hear what they were saying until I came closer. What I did see, though, was that Eric stuck his hand out to shake with the other man, who ignored the gesture.

By the time I'd come closer to the pair, their voices had risen considerably.

"You should have given me a heads-up. I had to read about your bankruptcy in the paper."

"It won't be a problem, Kevin, I promise. It's a formality I have to go through, according to my lawyer, but I'm going to pay you back every cent."

"Is that right?"

"Yes, that's right."

"Since when, Eric? You stopped making monthly payments even before Natalie died. I didn't press it after the crash, but it's been two years, and now you pull this stunt."

"You need to give me a little more time. My finances are going to improve in a big way very soon."

"Yeah, because all your debts will be forgiven. I want you to officially reaffirm the debt you owe me."

"Well, I'll have to talk to my lawyer about that."

"Always an excuse, huh, Eric? You just told me you were going to pay, so why not make it official?"

"I'll have to see about it. My lawyer's handling everything."

"You can't palm this off on your lawyer, partner. You agreed to buy my share of the business. I was fool enough to let you do it over time. I did you a favor, and now you're backing out of the deal," Kevin shouted.

In the floodlights that illuminated the parking lot, the two men eyed each other warily. I noticed that Kevin had balled his hands into fists.

"I intend to pay you," Eric repeated, "but I already told you, I can't reaffirm any debts without consulting my lawyer."

"Can't or won't?" Kevin said belligerently.

"All right. Won't. Is that clear enough for you?"

"Crystal clear," Kevin said, as he swung his right fist upwards, connecting solidly with Eric's jaw.

Clutching his injury, Eric stepped back, dazed, before advancing. Flailing his arms wildly, he tried, without success, to land a punch.

In the meantime, Kevin struck a couple more blows, throwing Eric off balance. He struggled to regain his footing but landed on the ground, instead. Kevin jumped on top of his adversary and began pummeling him, but, this time, Eric managed to land a few punches of his own.

"Kevin, if you don't stop this right now, I'm going to call the cops!" said a tall woman wearing a black leather motorcycle jacket and boots.

To my amazement, both men stopped fighting, stood up, and dusted themselves off.

"Sorry, Gina," Eric muttered.

"You ought to be ashamed of yourselves!" she scolded. She glared at the crowd that had gathered. "Excitement's over. Nothing to see here." Turning back to Kevin, she said, "Come on; our table's ready, and I haven't waited here an hour to skip dinner. Let's go!"

As Kevin followed his wife, Eric watched, rubbing his jaw.

At the restaurant's entrance, Kevin paused, glowering at Eric. "You haven't heard the last of this! Not by a long shot!" he yelled.

Eric made a dismissive gesture, but he was obviously upset. Looking around, he noticed me for the first time. "Hi, Amanda. I don't much feel like having dinner after that. I'm afraid I wouldn't be very good company. Tell Susan I'll get in touch with her in a couple of days."

Without waiting for an answer, he hopped into his truck, backed out of his parking space, and peeled out of the lot.

Chapter 5

When I told Susan about the scene I'd witnessed in the parking lot, she said, "I'm tempted to call Eric right now, but I know it won't do any good. He's a brooder. I'd better wait until he calls me. Do you think he's hurt?"

"Probably not seriously, but I think he's going to be sore for several days."

"I assume Kevin threw the first punch."

"You're right. I think he took Eric by surprise. Even though they were arguing, Eric didn't act as though he thought they might come to blows."

"Kevin always was a hothead. He and Eric used to be partners, but then Kevin decided he wanted out. It was before Natalie died, but, even at the time, the business wasn't doing very well. Eric insisted he could make a go of it on his own, so he agreed to buy Kevin's share."

"From what they said, it sounded as though Eric hasn't made any payments for a really long time, and, coincidentally, I happened to find out today that Eric's in debt to Greg Winters, too."

Susan frowned. "Name sounds familiar."

"I think you met him when we were at the spring arts and

crafts fair. He and his wife Rebecca sing in the Lonesome Valley Pioneers Choir."

"Isn't he the guy who sang 'Ghost Rider in the Sky' that day?"

"That's the one."

"It sent shivers up my spine. He has a great voice. He seemed like a nice man. I hope he's not going to duke it out with Eric, too."

"I doubt it. Greg's hyper safety conscious and worried about crime. I can't imagine he'd get into a physical fight with Eric. Besides, they're related—some kind of distant cousins—so he may be more forgiving than Kevin; Greg's really angry, though, according to Rebecca."

"Evidently, Eric's in pretty deep. I hope he's right that things are going to turn around for him soon. The guy just can't seem to catch a break."

Susan's concern about Eric's situation distracted her during our dinner, which also turned out to be somewhat disappointing culinary-wise. The food and the service were nothing special, and ambiance was nonexistent. After dinner, we declined dessert and decided that we'd scratch the place off our list. I suggested a do-over at Miguel's the following Sunday, and Susan readily agreed.

I didn't see Susan again until Saturday, when we were both scheduled to work in the Roadrunner's booth at the high school's winter craft fair.

I began to understand how popular the fundraiser was when I had to park several blocks away from the high school. Concession booths run by local organizations lined the wide hallway that led to the gym. The goodies tempted me, but I decided to wait until I left to make my purchases. Belle had already come and gone, having helped set up the Library

Auxiliary's tables and worked the morning shift.

The gym buzzed with activity, and I didn't see the Roadrunner's space right away, but when I started walking down the first aisle, I spotted it at the very end.

"Wow! I can't believe how busy it is," I whispered to a harried Susan between customers. "This is crazy." I pitched in to help bag the gifts of art that eager customers had selected.

"It comes in waves," she said, as a high schooler dressed in a band uniform approached with her purchase.

I'd noticed several other band members on my way in, so I asked the student whether the band was performing for the crafts show crowd.

"Oh, no. We have practice in a few minutes out on the field." She flashed a smile before disappearing through the crowd.

The Roadrunner had booked a triple space, so that we had room to display paintings on a portable grid in the back. There was a table on either side, one with boxes of prints and our checkout area, the other laden with jewelry, pottery, and note cards.

I soon learned what Susan meant by waves. Our booth cleared out for a few minutes, ending the crush I'd seen when I'd come in.

"Hey, Beautiful!" I instantly recognized the voice. Even if I hadn't, only one man in the world had the habit of casually addressing me as "Beautiful." Susan's twenty-five-year-old nephew Chip loved to flirt, especially with older women. When I'd first met him, I'd taken him seriously, but I'd soon learned not to.

"Hi, Chip. Have you been here all morning?"

"Yup. I helped set up. I volunteered for the early shift since I can't stay all day."

I knew what he meant. Although Chip was a talented painter, his art career hadn't really taken off, and he worked in his father's pizza parlor. Since Saturday tended to be the busiest for pizza deliveries, I figured he'd have to leave to go to work before the show closed at five.

Chip handed Susan a bottle of water.

She uncapped it and took a sip.

"Water, Amanda?" Chip offered, holding out the other bottle he had. "I can go get another one now while we're not busy."

"Well. OK. Thank you," I said, accepting the bottle. Selling art and eating didn't mix, any more than selling art and sipping soft drinks or coffee. The possibility of spilling them was greater when our venue was as active as this one, so water was our go-to drink during busy shows.

I had the chance to take a couple of sips before we were slammed again. I sold a necklace to a young mother, several packets of artists' Christmas cards to a white-haired couple, and a large painting to a dentist who was looking for something to decorate her reception room. By the time Chip came back, we'd fallen into another trough.

"You certainly timed that right," Susan told her nephew, who grinned in response.

"I see an empty spot on the grid," he commented. "You must have sold Pamela's tiger portrait. I'd better go grab another painting to replace it. Aunt Susan?"

She reached into her pocket, produced her car keys, and handed them to Chip. "Let's display Ralph's desert landscape. It's in my trunk."

With a quick nod, Chip left to get the painting. When he returned, he carried it high above his head to avoid close encounters with the crowd. He carefully hung it on the grid and stepped back to make sure it aligned perfectly with the other paintings.

"Looks like we're doing all right," Chip said.

"This is always a busy show," Susan agreed.

"I wish I were so busy," I said wistfully. "Last night was the first time I haven't had even one visitor for my studio tour, and I haven't sold a painting at the Roadrunner in three weeks."

"Things will pick up," Susan, ever the optimist, assured me.

"I sure hope so," I said glumly. I hadn't meant to indulge in a pity party for myself, but after reviewing my finances the previous evening, I admit I'd felt a bit panicky. I told myself to get a grip. My friends, especially Susan, didn't need to be exposed to my distress. She had enough on her plate worrying about Eric's dire financial situation. I wondered whether he'd called her, as he'd promised. I was about to ask her when another crowd inundated us, and it took us half an hour to handle the rush.

When I came up for air, I saw that Chip was talking with a young couple in front of a booth in the corner of the gym.

"There's a coincidence," Susan noted, looking toward Chip. "I don't recognize the girl, but Chip went to high school with Josh. He's Eric's nephew."

"How is Eric? He seemed embarrassed after the dust-up with his former partner."

"Coping, I suppose. He apologized for standing us up. He insisted again that he had something he wanted to show me, but he wouldn't give me any hint about what it is. I told him I could stop by around eight tomorrow evening. I plan on dropping by after our dinner at Miguel's, but I didn't mention it, especially since my first dinner invitation didn't work out too well."

Several people came into the booth then, and we turned our attention to them. The reprieve between waves had clocked in at a scant minute or two. Finally, the rush subsided.

"I hate to tell you this, but I'm going to have to leave for work," Chip said, glancing at his phone.

"Sure. No problem," Susan said. "We're only open for another hour, and Frank's going to come by to help pack up and take the paintings back to the Roadrunner. Say, wasn't that Josh you were talking to?"

"Sure was. I haven't seen him in a while. We're going to the Suns' game in Phoenix next week. Somebody gave him a couple of tickets, and his girlfriend Kayla doesn't want to go. I'm sure Dad won't mind giving me one night off."

"He'll wish he was the one to get the free tickets—that's for sure."

"Well, I should get on the road." Chip winked at me. "Bye, now, Beautiful."

I smiled at his nonsense and briefly wondered whether Brian thought I was beautiful. He'd never said so, but he had told me he thought I was "amazing."

I didn't have time to think about it anymore, because Frank showed up just then, and I took the opportunity to visit the food booths in the hallway before they totally sold out of goodies. I found Rebecca at the choir's table, which, fortunately, looked very well stocked. Some of the other tables were practically empty.

"You're in luck," Rebecca told me. "We just brought in more goodies. If we don't constantly replenish our treats, we'd sell out way before the fair ends."

"Good idea. I have to have some of that peppermint fudge. It's Emma's favorite. And, let's see, one of those carrot bars, a gingerbread man, a couple brownies, and the big tin of chocolate walnut fudge. That's the same kind as you made for the cookie exchange, isn't it?"

"The very same," Rebecca assured me.

"I'm going to freeze the candy, so I'll have it when the family comes, but the rest is for me," I confessed. "I'm going to try to be good and ration them, though."

"It's hard, isn't it? I can't resist temptation this time of year. Do you want to pick this up on your way home? I can hold it for you."

"Thanks, Rebecca, but I'd better take it with me now. It's going to be chaos when we break down our booths at five, and you'll probably be able to finish before we will."

Rebecca neatly stacked the treats I'd bought in a large paper bag with handles, and I returned to the Roadrunner's booth to find another surge of activity. Unfortunately, the buying frenzy didn't include either of my two paintings that were on display, so we'd be hauling those back to the gallery soon.

We were still checking out customers when the five o'clock closing time rolled around, but slowly the gym emptied, leaving only the vendors to pack up their goods and remove their displays. Pamela and her husband Rich showed up to help, and we were able to pack up and load Frank's truck in record time. Pamela told Susan and me we didn't need to come back to the gallery. They planned to unload quickly and sort things out the following morning.

Susan and I were both happy to be on the way home. She'd been there longer than I had, and we both felt tired. "I'm going to call Chip and order a pizza," she told me. "I'm too exhausted to cook. How about you?"

"I have leftovers from last night's dinner. I'll just pop them into the microwave."

As we exited the gym, we noticed that quite a few people were still milling about in the hallway, and a couple of food vendors were selling their snacks at half price.

When we left the building, we heard a siren in the distance. Maybe the throng hovering around the entrance expected to catch a glimpse of the emergency vehicle, but we didn't see any flashing red lights.

"Where did you park?" Susan asked when we'd made our way through the crowd.

"Over on Third Street. I couldn't find any place closer."

"Let me drop you off at your car," she offered.

"That would be great."

"I'm right over there," she said, pointing to her car, which was parked an aisle away.

I sank gratefully into the passenger seat and buckled my seat belt.

Susan backed up and swung into the lane leading to the street in front of the high school. The siren we'd noticed earlier had been growing louder and louder, and now we could see where it came from. An ambulance veered into the lane.

"Uh, oh. It's turning in here. I hope it's nothing too serious." Susan pulled her car over to the right of the lane as the emergency vehicle sped past us.

"I hope not," I replied. We both turned and saw the ambulance stop in front of the high school's entrance.

No sooner than it stopped, we were startled to hear another siren, and before we knew it, a second ambulance had turned into the lane.

We looked at each other with concern.

"What in the world is going on?" I asked as more flashing red lights appeared in the distance.

Chapter 6

"Rebecca's still inside. Maybe she knows what happened." I pulled my cell phone out of my bag, scrolled through my contacts, and punched in her number. She answered immediately.

"We saw the ambulances," I said, as soon as Rebecca answered. "What's going on? Was there an accident?" I turned on my phone's speaker so that Susan could hear Rebecca, too.

"I'm not sure. The EMTs are going into the band room now. Oh, I hope everyone is going to be all right. We had such a wonderful turnout, and people really enjoyed the fair. I'll call you if I hear any news. Someone must know what happened."

"OK, thanks, Rebecca. We're keeping our fingers crossed that it turns out not to be too serious." I put my phone back into my bag.

"We should go," Susan said. "I'd better get the car out of the way before the ambulances come back."

Susan dropped me off at my car on Third Street, but, before she left, she asked me to let her know if I found out about the emergency that brought the ambulances to the high school, and I assured her I would.

When I pulled into my carport, I realized that I'd forgotten to leave any lights on in the house. I didn't like coming home to a dark house, but Laddie was waiting to greet me on the other side of the door. I quickly flipped the light switch, and my little home felt as cozy as ever. Mona Lisa jumped down from her kitty tree and ran to me, vying with Laddie for my attention. They both acted a little needier than usual, but I soon realized the reason: it was past their normal dinnertime, and they wanted to eat right away. I set the paper bag containing the cookies and candy I'd bought on the counter, took my coat off, and filled their bowls before I heated the remains of last night's casserole for myself. While it warmed in the oven, I made room in my freezer for the candy. After some rearranging, I was able to close the freezer door. I put my baked goods into the cookie jar, except for the carrot bar, which I decided would make a good dessert. It was piled high with cream cheese frosting, one of my favorites.

I'd just polished off dinner and dessert when my cell phone rang. I fished for it in my bag, picked it up, and saw that Rebecca was calling.

"It's awful," she began, before choking back a sob.

My heart sank, and I held my breath while I waited for her to continue.

"They took my neighbor Carmen and two band members to the hospital. Some guy from the county health department suspects they have food poisoning, but that's not the worst of it. He found out that all three of them bought carrot bars from the Pioneers. I still don't believe it. I know every one of the choir members who made treats for us to sell, and they're all reliable people. This is the tenth year we've had a booth. It just doesn't seem possible."

"Carrot bars?" I croaked. "I just ate one of them!"

"Did they have little carrots piped in orange and green frosting on the top?"

"No, just cream cheese frosting."

"And you bought it sometime around four, if I remember right, not in the last half hour."

"That's right."

"You bought different bars than the ones that made the kids and Carmen sick. We always replenish our stock about half an hour before the fair's due to close. We sold only the decorated bars after that. The funny thing is—well, it's not funny, but odd—that nobody knew who made them. Mary made the bars with plain cream cheese frosting, but she didn't decorate any of her carrot bars."

Despite Rebecca's reassurances, I felt a bit queasy at the mere thought of possible food poisoning.

"I can't understand how this happened," Rebecca wailed. "I really can't. I've spoken to everybody who made treats to sell at our booth, and they all brought exactly what they signed up to bring. I know for sure Mary didn't make the decorated bars because I saw her bring in the plain ones myself, and then she left. She couldn't help at the booth this year because her husband's recovering from a stroke at home, and she needs to be with him most of the time until he can manage better on his own."

"How did the man from the health department figure out the problem was with the carrot bars so quickly?"

"He asked Carmen and the band members if they had eaten anything there, and the bars are the only thing they ate. I remember selling one to Carmen myself. I feel so guilty."

"There's no way you could have known she'd get food poisoning from it."

"I know, but I still feel really bad. When the EMTs wheeled her out on a gurney to the ambulance, she was wearing an oxygen mask. Greg and I are going to head over to the hospital in a few minutes to see how she's doing."

"Please wish her well for me and let me know how she's getting along."

"I will. I promise."

No sooner had I set my cell phone down than Laddie ran to the kitchen door, whipping his tail back and forth in eager anticipation. He jumped up and down on his front paws when I opened the door, and Belle came in and handed me a green plastic-wrapped bag.

"Divinity," she said, stopping to pet Laddie, who followed us into the living room after I thanked Belle and set the candy on the counter.

"Are you feeling all right, Amanda? You look a little pale."

"I'm OK, but, for a minute, I was afraid I had food poisoning." I explained that Susan and I had seen three ambulances coming to the high school just as we'd left and told her what Rebecca had said.

"Food poisoning from carrot bars? I've never heard of such a thing, have you?"

"No, I can't say that I have."

"Were there any left in the choir's booth that the health department can test?"

"That's a good question. I'll have to ask Rebecca when she calls me back."

"I hope they can isolate the cause. What if more people ate them?'

"I suppose they'll put out some kind of recall announcement."

"Let's hope word gets out before more people get sick. This is a terrible end to a great day. Our library auxiliary always does really well at the high school fair."

"The Roadrunner had a good day, too. I just hope nobody's seriously ill. Rebecca said Carmen was on oxygen when they took her to the hospital."

"Poor Carmen. At the party, she said she was really looking forward to buying gifts at the fair, remember?"

I nodded. Rebecca's neighbor had gone from a fun day purchasing unique hand-crafted gifts for her family and friends to the hospital. It was truly horrific. For the rest of the evening, I kept expecting Rebecca to call me with an update on Carmen's condition, but the phone never rang.

Chapter 7

As soon as I woke, I checked my phone right away for messages, but there weren't any. It was around six o'clock, and I knew Rebecca didn't usually get up that early, but her husband Greg did. The only problem was that I didn't have Greg's cell phone number, only Rebecca's.

I thought I might be able to catch him at the little park where we both walked our dogs, though. I called Laddie, snapped his leash onto his collar, and we departed for a walk before breakfast. Laddie pranced along happily beside me, the cold air not bothering him in the least, but I shivered as I pulled the knit cap I wore down over my ears and fastened the hood of my parka over it, pulling it tight under my chin. A cold wind blew from the north, and normally I would have been tempted to skip our walk because of it, but I was hoping to see Greg and find out how Carmen was getting along.

When we arrived at the park, we found it deserted, except for Greg, who was walking Skippy and Tucker. As soon as he saw Laddie and me, he hurried toward us. The terriers yapped with excitement at seeing Laddie, as they hustled to greet him.

"Greg, what happened with Carmen last night? Is she OK? Rebecca was going to call me to let me know."

"Yeah, sorry, Amanda. We didn't really know anything until late last night, when it was too late to call, anyway. Carmen's still in the hospital. Rebecca's staying with the kids until Carmen's husband Lew comes home." He pointed to a house across the street, a couple doors down from his. "They live right over there. The kids came to the hospital with Lew last night, and, by midnight, they were pretty well exhausted, so Rebecca took them home, while Lew stayed at the hospital. I hung out with him for a while, until he was able to talk to the doctor. Carmen's really been through the mill, but she and the kids in the band will get through it, according to the doc. He said they were poisoned, and the health department's analyzing the carrot bars that hadn't been sold yet. Rebecca's fit to be tied. We have no idea how this could have happened."

Since Greg and I were the only people stirring in the neighborhood, we noticed immediately when a white painter's van with a ladder secured to its side parked in front of the house Greg had pointed out earlier.

A man wearing a navy hoodie and jeans jumped out. When Greg waved to him, he came over to us.

"Lew, how's Carmen this morning?"

"Exhausted. She finally went to sleep a little while ago, so I came home to regroup. I'll take the kids back to the hospital to see her later this morning."

"I met Carmen at Rebecca's cookie exchange. I was so sorry to hear what happened," I told Lew.

"Pardon me," Greg said. "I should have introduced you two. Amanda Trent, Lew Hearndon."

"Hi, Amanda. Aren't you the artist? I think Carmen mentioned that you were going to be at the fair."

"Yes. I was there, all afternoon, to help at the Roadrunner's booth."

"I'm still trying to wrap my head around the fact that Carmen and the band kids were poisoned at the fair. I can't understand how it happened, but the guy from the health department was really concerned. He told me he was going to alert the media to warn people."

"We hope nobody else has a problem," Greg said.

"That's for sure. I wouldn't wish this on my worst enemy. See you later."

"I should get going, too," Greg said. "Rebecca'll be coming home in a minute. She plans to go over her list of everybody who provided baked goods or candy for the Pioneers' booth and try to figure out where those carrot bars came from."

"I thought Rebecca already did that."

"She did, but it can't hurt to take another look. Who knows? Maybe we'll come up with something. I guarantee you, somebody knows where those poison carrot bars came from, but whoever it is probably doesn't want to admit it. I think the person who made them mixed in some ingredients by mistake."

"I suppose that could have happened," I said, although I thought it unlikely. "Anyway, I'm relieved to hear that Carmen and the band members will be all right."

By the time Laddie and I walked the few blocks home, I felt like an icicle. Laddie hadn't minded the cold one bit, but my teeth chattered until I warmed myself by drinking a cup of strong, hot tea while Mona Lisa playfully batted my feet.

Laddie had received his share of attention, and now she wanted hers. After I'd warmed up, I flicked her feather toy back and forth for her so that she could try to catch it. By the time I ended the game, she seemed satisfied, leaping to the top of her kitty tree and surveying Laddie and me from on high.

I decided it would be a perfect day to complete my portrait

of Mr. Big, because Belle and Dennis were spending the day in Prescott with Belle's cousin. I'd offered to dogsit Mr. Big, but they'd decided to take him along. With several uninterrupted hours available for me to paint, I could complete the portrait without having to worry about hiding it from Belle.

I donned an old flannel shirt, rolled up the sleeves, and went to work. Laddie cooperated nicely, curling up on his bed in the corner of my studio and taking a nap. Although my uninterrupted painting schedule wasn't strictly uninterrupted—I broke for lunch and, later, to play fetch in the backyard with Laddie—I worked steadily and felt a sense of accomplishment when, with a flourish, I added my artist's signature at the bottom of Mr. Big's portrait. I left the painting on an easel in the middle of the studio since Belle wouldn't be coming over in the evening.

I was looking forward to dinner at Miguel's with Susan, my queasiness from the night before, caused by the thought that I might have eaten a poisoned carrot bar, all but forgotten. I showered, styled my hair with the help of my blow dryer, and put on some make-up. The cold north wind hadn't let up since Laddie and I had taken our morning walk to the park, so I decided to wear my warmest sweater with jeans and knee-high boots.

After I fed Laddie and Mona Lisa, I grabbed my car keys and was out the door. Unfortunately, I didn't get very far.

The clicking sound when I turned my key in the ignition told me all I needed to know. I wasn't going anywhere.

Chapter 8

I groaned and rested my head on the steering wheel for a couple of seconds. I tried to remember the last time I replaced the battery in my SUV before recalling that I never had. Another unexpected expense, I thought, as I went back inside, surprising Laddie and Mona Lisa.

There was no time to wait for help from the auto club without being late for dinner, so I called Susan, who volunteered to pick me up.

Laddie waited at my side, while I watched for her from the front window. Mona Lisa showed no interest in my impending departure and crept behind the sofa, one of her favorite hiding spots.

When Susan pulled up in front of the house, I left my disappointed retriever behind and scurried outside to meet her.

"Thanks for picking me up."

"No problem. When we get back after dinner, we can try to start your car again. I have jumper cables."

"Really? You know how to use those? I wouldn't have a clue."

"I do. They've come in handy more than once."

"It's worth a shot, I guess." If it worked, I could put off buying another battery.

"Have you heard anything more about the poisonings?" Susan asked me. I'd called to let her know what I'd learned from Rebecca and Greg earlier, so she was in the loop.

"No, nothing except that I heard about the carrot bars, or a warning about them, on the radio news this morning."

"It was also on TV. I sure hope the health department people can figure out what's going on."

"Me, too. Poor Carmen and the band members! What a way to end the fair."

When we arrived at Miguel's, we found it humming but not so crowded that we had to wait very long for a table. After ten minutes or so, the hostess escorted us to a cozy two-seater booth tucked away in a corner. Colorful pottery and figurines, all handcrafted in Mexico, occupied alcoves in the adobe walls where Diego Rivera prints hung. Recorded mariachi music sounded in the background, but it wasn't so loud that it made conversation difficult.

As soon as we were seated, our server appeared with a bowl of corn chips and smaller bowls of salsa and bean dip. I ordered a margarita, while Susan settled for a diet cola. We barely glanced at the menus the hostess had given us, because we'd dined there so many times before. As usual, Susan ordered the house special, shrimp tacos. I waffled between fajitas and enchiladas, finally deciding on the fajitas, which would come on a sizzling platter, along with sides of rice and beans and generous dollops of guacamole and sour cream.

While we waited for our meals, we munched on the chips and sipped our drinks.

"I promised I'd stop by Eric's place after dinner, but it shouldn't take too long," Susan reminded me.

"OK. I can wait in the car."

"No, please come in with me. I'm sure he won't mind."

"Well, I don't know if I should. He might not appreciate it."

"To tell you the truth, I don't want to be alone with him. I like him, but only as a friend. When I saw him last year, he made a pass at me. It was awkward for both of us. I could never think of him as anything but Natalie's husband. He may have been drinking before that incident, but, still, it wouldn't hurt to have backup."

"All right. Safety in numbers, I guess."

"Exactly."

After dinner, Susan drove to Eric's house, which was in a quiet neighborhood. Other than a couple walking their beagle, we were the only people outside. Christmas lights twinkled on several of the houses, but no lights were visible in front of Eric's place, nor were there any emanating from inside.

"Hmm. Maybe he's not home," Susan noted. "I'll give him a quick call." She waited while the phone on the other end rang several times before she gave up.

"He could have his phone turned off," I said. "Look, there's kind of a glow over at the side of the house. He could be home."

"Might as well check, now that we're here."

We got out of the car and climbed the few steps to the front porch. Susan rang Eric's doorbell, but there was no answer.

"I can hear something in there," Susan told me. "It sounds like the TV's on."

"Let's check the side window. That's where the light's coming from."

We went around to the corner and peeked into the window. Susan had been right: on the wall, a flat screen television blared.

She saw the figure on the floor before I did. She clutched my arm. "Look! Over by the desk."

Eric was sprawled on the floor beside the desk. As far as I could tell, he wasn't moving.

Susan tapped the windowpane and called to him, but he didn't respond.

My hands trembled as I reached for my cell phone and dialed 9-1-1.

"A man's collapsed!" I told the emergency operator.

"Is he breathing?"

"I don't know. We're outside, and he's inside. We can see him through a window, but we can't get in. The house is locked." At least, I assumed it was locked, but I went around to the front door, anyway, just to make sure.

"Address?"

"7-9-2," I read the metal numbers beside the front door. "I don't know the name of the street." I looked at Susan, who shook her head. She was so rattled that she couldn't think of it, either. "We'll have to check the street sign," I told the operator.

Susan ran to the dog walkers on the other side of the street. At first, they looked at her as though she were a crazy woman, but she finally made them understand that it was an emergency involving their neighbor, and they followed her back to Eric's porch.

"Copper Valley Road," Susan said breathlessly, and I relayed the street name to the operator.

As we waited for help to arrive, Susan led the couple around the side of the porch, and they were shocked to see Eric lying motionless on the floor inside.

"I'll try the back door," the man said, vaulting over the porch rail and disappearing around the side of the house. He returned in a minute to report that the back door was locked, too.

We heard the wail of sirens, and the beagle began to bay. The man tried to shush him, but the little dog didn't stop until the sirens did.

A patrol officer approached first, followed by a pair of EMTs.

The policeman had evidently gotten the word that he'd have to break in, but he tried the door, anyway. When it didn't budge, the cop bashed in the side light window with his baton, reached inside, and unlocked the front door. He pushed it open and flipped a light switch. The EMTs followed him, and the four of us were right behind them. We went through the living room into the den where Eric lay on the floor. The police officer grabbed the remote and turned off the blaring television while the paramedics knelt to check on Eric. We held our breaths while they examined him.

"We're too late," one of them announced.

Susan started to sob.

"I'm sorry. Are you relatives?"" he asked.

"No, just friends," I responded.

"We're neighbors," the woman dog walker said. Holding their beagle, her husband stood beside her. The hound wiggled, but he held onto it.

The patrol officer huddled with the EMTs, while Susan tried to control her crying.

"Poor Eric," she murmured. "He's only forty-five."

"Could be a heart attack or a stroke, maybe," the neighbor speculated. "We didn't know him too well, but he seemed like a good guy."

"Folks, I'm going to have to ask you to wait until my sergeant gets here and we can sort things out."

"Do they know what happened?" I asked, nodding toward the paramedics.

"No. The coroner will have to determine the cause of death. Now, if you all wouldn't mind waiting in the kitchen—"

As we walked past Eric's desk, I noticed a neat stack of papers, held together by an oversize clip, on top. I craned my neck as we passed by, but I couldn't read the document, although I noticed that the paper was longer than regular printer paper. Susan looked at it, too, but we couldn't stop to examine it because the officer kept urging us to go into the kitchen.

The den was separated from the kitchen by a breakfast bar counter. When we walked around the side of it, I saw a gray marble-topped island in the center of the room. But it wasn't the upscale carrara-topped island that grabbed my attention.

It was what lay on top of it.

Chapter 9

A single carrot bar decorated with neatly piped orange and green icing in the shape of a carrot surrounded by crumbs sat on a plate in the center of the island, next to a half-full mug of coffee.

"Oh, no! Eric must have been poisoned!" Susan exclaimed.

"It certainly looks that way," I agreed.

The neighborhood couple looked at us in confusion.

"Why do you think that?" the man asked.

"There was an incident at the high school yesterday. Three people were taken to the hospital, and they'd all eaten carrot bars just like that." I pointed to the innocent-looking dessert on the island. "Anyway, the health department says it was food poisoning. Warnings have been all over the news lately."

"We didn't hear a thing about it," the woman said. "We spent the day putting up our Christmas lights and decorating the house."

"Eric must not have heard about it, either," Susan said. "I should have called to warn him."

"There was no reason to think that Eric would eat any of these bars. I didn't see him at the fair, did you?"

"No. I'm sure he wasn't there. It's not the kind of event he'd go to, not without Natalie, anyway."

"So you can't blame yourself, Susan. It was an accident you couldn't possibly have anticipated."

"I suppose, but I still feel terrible."

"We need to tell the police officer."

"Tell me what?"

I whirled to see the officer coming into the kitchen. I pointed out the carrot bars, and he immediately understood the implication. Unlike the neighbors, he'd obviously heard the latest news.

"OK. I'll alert the coroner. You folks just stay put, and don't touch anything. It shouldn't be too much longer."

The beagle wiggled impatiently. He wanted to get down, but the neighbor man held onto him. Despite his firm grip, the dog managed to lurch toward the countertop.

"Watch out, Jack!" his wife warned.

"Let's wait outside," Jack said.

"The police officer said to wait here," his wife protested, but she followed him.

We heard voices and a door closing.

From the numerous crumbs remaining on the plate, I surmised that Eric must have eaten several carrot bars. Whatever the quantity, it had evidently been enough to be lethal. I shuddered to think that Carmen and the two band members could have suffered the same fate as Eric, had they'd eaten more carrot bars.

"Well, well, well. Who have we here? If it isn't the Bobbsey twins," a gruff voice said.

I could tell by the startled, yet resigned, expression on Susan's face that she was experiencing a déjà-vu moment. For that matter, so was I. Susan and I had been together when we'd discovered a body several months earlier, and Lieutenant Belmont, the same detective, had investigated the case. He'd treated us both like suspects and had even arrested Susan, so I knew she would have preferred to avoid seeing the lieutenant, but the grouchy detective and I had come to a sort of grudging truce after an uneasy collaboration on a murder case in September. I hadn't encountered the lieutenant since, and I was surprised to see him back at work, because he'd just had heart bypass surgery at the time.

I ignored his sarcastic remark and pointed to the plate sitting on the island's countertop. "Look at that. He must have eaten more than one of those carrot bars," I observed.

"Still playing Nancy Drew, are we, Mrs. Trent?"

"Haven't you heard of the food poisoning at the high school yesterday?"

"Don't be ridiculous. Of course, I know about it. What are you two doing here, anyway?"

Susan took a deep breath before explaining that Eric had invited her to come to the house because he wanted to show her something but that he hadn't told her what it was.

"Why were you here?" Lieutenant Belmont asked me bluntly.

"I came along for the ride, literally. My car wouldn't start, and Susan and I were going out to dinner, so she picked me up, and here we are."

"Enough," the lieutenant held up his hand, much like a traffic cop signaling a driver to stop. All of a sudden, he sounded quite weary. "You can come down to the station tomorrow and give your statement to Sergeant Martinez."

"Are you feeling all right, lieutenant?" I asked. "I'm surprised to see you back at work so soon."

"I'm fine," he snapped, before relenting slightly. "There's only so much TV a man can watch. I came back to work last week. Now, you two go home. I've got work to do."

Without hesitation, we exited Eric's house by the front door.

"It figures *he* would be the one to investigate," Susan groused.

"You probably won't have to see him again. He told us Dave Martinez would be taking our statements. You know, Dawn's husband." Dawn, a clay artist, was a member of the Roadrunner.

"Oh, right. Dave's a nice guy. Too bad he has to work with Belmont."

"They actually get along pretty well. I think Dave's the only cop at the police station who's sort of a buddy of the lieutenant. I know Dave and Dawn kept tabs on him the whole time he was recovering from surgery. I think maybe the lieutenant got in too much of a hurry to return to work. He looks pale to me."

"You're way more charitable toward him than I am. I'll never forgive him for putting me in jail."

"I know it was terrible." Even though I'd observed a few cracks in his gruff exterior, I couldn't blame Susan a bit for feeling as she did. Her arrest had been completely unjustified, and even though it had happened many months ago, it wasn't something she'd ever be likely to forget, especially since she'd had to stay overnight in the county jail.

A small crowd of neighbors had gathered across the street, joined by the couple with the beagle. Next door, to the left, a family of five watched the scene from their porch while, on the other side, a woman had pulled her curtains aside to catch the action at Eric's place.

The coroner's van was parked in front of Susan's car, and a

couple of police cruisers were in back of it. The patrol officer who'd arrived first on the scene was standing next to one of the cruisers, talking to another cop. As a red Mustang zipped past, pulled into Eric's driveway, and screeched to a sudden halt, we all watched to see who had arrived.

Although I'd never met them, I recognized the pair immediately as Eric's nephew Josh and his girlfriend Kayla.

"What's wrong?" Josh shouted to the policeman.

Without waiting for an answer, Josh grabbed Kayla's hand and pulled her toward the front door, but the policeman moved quickly to block their entrance.

"Sorry, sir. You can't go in there."

"This is my uncle's house. I want to see him now!" Josh demanded, his voice raised in agitation.

"I can't let you do that, sir. Now, if you'll just wait over there, by your car, I'll let the detective know you're here, and you can speak to him."

"Detective? What's going on? Where's my uncle?"

"Come on, Josh," Kayla urged. She tugged at his arm, but he refused to budge.

"I'm not going anywhere until I find out what's happened," Josh declared.

Then he noticed the next-door neighbor watching him from behind her curtain. "What are you looking at?" he yelled. "You witch!" She disappeared from view as the curtain fell back into place.

"Josh," Susan called, beckoning him to come over to where we were standing, next to her car.

"Ms. Carpenter." On seeing Susan, Josh took it down a notch. "Do you know why the cops are here?"

"Yes, I do, Josh. It's your Uncle Eric. We found him on the

floor in the den a little while ago. I'm so sorry to tell you, but Eric's dead."

"No way!" Josh protested. "That can't be. He was fine when we stopped by last night after the fair."

"You didn't happen to bring him anything from the fair, did you?"

"I did," Kayla said. "He loves carrot bars, and I saw some cute ones at the Pioneers' booth right when we were on our way out. I picked up a few for him."

Kayla noticed that Susan and I exchanged an ah-ha look.

"What? Did I do something wrong?"

Chapter 10

"There's no way you could have known," I explained, "but, according to the health department, decorated carrot bars from the fair caused food poisoning. Three people who ate them were taken to the hospital yesterday."

Kayla's face crumpled, and she burst into tears. "I killed Josh's uncle," she wailed.

Josh pulled her into his arms and tried to comfort her.

"It wasn't your fault," he said. "But it sure is somebody's fault. I want to know who made those carrot bars and how they ended up at the fair!"

"That's exactly what we want to know, too." Lieutenant Belmont had come outside to investigate the commotion.

He looked at Susan and me with disapproval. "I thought you two would be long gone by now. Get out of here. Scoot!"

Although I didn't appreciate his tone or his patronizing attitude, we complied, leaving Josh and Kayla to deal with the lieutenant's questions.

It wasn't until I went to bed, snuggling under my fluffy comforter, with Laddie stretched out across my feet and Mona Lisa curled up on her pillow next to me, that I realized both Susan and I had completely forgotten about using her jumper cables to try to start my SUV. I made a mental note to call the auto club in the morning before falling to sleep and dreaming about carrot bars decorated with a black skull and crossbones contrasting with garish carrot-orange frosting. Not nearly the sweet dreams of sugarplums that I'd had a few days before.

When I woke up the next morning, I had a headache. Laddie sensed my distress and anxiously leaned in close to me while Mona Lisa, oblivious, meowed loudly, demanding I serve her breakfast.

I reassured Laddie with a hug and some soothing words, put on my robe, and accompanied my crew to the kitchen. I put the kettle on to boil before I dished out breakfast at opposite ends of the kitchen for my furry companions. After drinking a couple of cups of strong black breakfast tea, I felt my headache begin to dissipate.

I turned on my cell phone, which I always switched off at night to avoid being awakened by a chiming notification, and saw that Belle had texted me after I'd gone to bed, leaving me the message that she and Dennis had opted to stay overnight in Prescott but would be back by noon today. I decided to wait until they returned to tell Belle about the shocking news of Eric's death, caused by the poisoned dessert bars.

I hadn't forgotten that the lieutenant had directed me to go to the police station to make a witness statement, but before I could drive anywhere, I needed to get my SUV started. After calling the auto club and learning that it would be a forty-five-minute wait until someone from their local contracted garage showed up, I hurriedly dressed and took Laddie for a quick walk in the neighborhood.

Several minutes after we returned, the mechanic showed up. After I explained that the car wouldn't start, he hooked up a battery tester to diagnose the problem.

"Deader than a door nail," he announced cheerfully.

I felt far from cheerful myself at this not-exactly-unexpected news.

"I can replace it for you. A new battery comes with a three-year warranty."

"OK. How much?" I asked, not that it mattered. I needed a battery and, although I might save some money if I asked Dennis to drive me to the auto parts store when he got off work and help me install it, I didn't want to wait.

After the mechanic told me what the damages came to, I reluctantly handed over my credit card, and, when he'd finished installing the new battery and my car started as soon as I turned my key in the ignition, I decided it was worth it.

I could go to the police station, make my statement, and shop for groceries on the way home, all before noon.

Sergeant Martinez was standing at the counter in the reception area, talking to a couple of other uniformed officers when I arrived at the station.

"Hi, Amanda. Let's go back to the conference room." He grabbed a clipboard, and we went down the hall. I'd been in the drab interrogation room before, but this room was different. It actually looked more like a conference room in a business office, with a large rectangular table dominating the space, rather than a prison cell.

He sat across from me and handed me the clipboard. "Just write down everything that happened last night, starting from the time you arrived at Eric Thompson's house. I'll type it up for you to sign, and you can be on your way. If Bill has any questions, I'm sure he'll be in touch."

"I'm sure he will."

Dave laughed as I rolled my eyes. At Dave's wife's request, I'd visited the grumpy lieutenant when he was in the hospital a few months back, and we all knew what an irascible character he was. To my knowledge, Dawn and Dave Martinez were the only friends Lieutenant Belmont had in the world.

"I'm surprised he's back at work already," I told Dave. "I thought he looked a little pale last night."

"Yeah, he's probably pushing it to come back this soon. He jumped the gun a little, most likely. When the chief found out he hadn't cleared it with his doctor, he insisted on written medical approval. That's why Bill isn't here this morning. He's at the doc's right now."

"Well, I hope it goes all right for him. He wasn't too cooperative while he was in the hospital, as I recall."

"You know Bill. He's stubborn, but if his doctor doesn't give him the all-clear, he won't have a choice. He'll be back on medical leave for a while, and that won't improve his mood any."

"No, I suppose not."

"Well, I'd better get back to the desk. Just bring me your statement when you're done."

As soon as Dave left, I began writing. I concentrated so that I wouldn't leave out any details. Dave had left the door ajar, and I could hear voices in the hallway a few times as people walked past, but it wasn't until a cell phone rang and I heard the chief answer it, right outside the conference room, that I set my pen down and paid attention.

"What's that you say? The poison's called coniine? I've never heard of it," He paused. "You're sure? Well, I'll be. This is a weird one."

He moved away from the door, his voice fading, as he continued with his phone conversation, until I heard a door close.

I reached into my bag, pulled out my cell phone, and searched for the word he'd mentioned. A dictionary definition popped up, and one word in it set off alarm bells immediately: "hemlock," the poison that killed the Greek philosopher Socrates! Other than that well-known case, I'd never heard of anyone who'd been poisoned with hemlock, but surely the chief had been talking to somebody at the health department or maybe the lab. I knew it had to relate to the case at hand.

Returning to my phone, I searched for cases of hemlock poisoning. A few reports mentioned that people had mistaken a hemlock root for a wild carrot. None of those incidents had happened in Arizona, as far as I could tell, but I did find out that both poison hemlock and water hemlock grew in Arizona. In fact, poison hemlock, if eaten, was one of the most toxic plants in the state.

"All set?"

I was so startled I dropped my phone. As it clattered on the tabletop, I smiled at Dave, trying to conceal my embarrassment at being caught fiddling with my phone when I should have been finishing my statement. "Just about. It shouldn't be more than a couple more minutes."

"OK," he said, easing into the chair opposite me. "Take your time."

I hurriedly scribbled my last paragraph while he waited patiently for me to finish. I don't think he noticed, but my hand was shaking the whole time.

Had someone innocently mistaken the poison roots for carrots, or had the poisonings been due to a far more sinister cause?

Chapter 11

By the time Dave had typed my statement and I'd signed it, the station buzzed with news about hemlock in the carrot bars. The chief had made no secret of the information he'd gleaned, and he told Dave to arrange for a press conference with a health department representative for later in the afternoon. Obviously, he thought that there was more upside than down to informing the public about the cause of Eric's death. I'd definitely have to watch the evening news to find out all the details, but I called Susan to give her a heads-up as soon as I left the station.

"Hemlock? I don't understand how something like that could get into dessert bars."

I explained about the possibility of the poison hemlock plant's root being mistaken for an edible vegetable. Actually, that probably wasn't as far-fetched as it had seemed at first to me. Lots of people—well, maybe not lots, but many—foraged for wild plants, whether to take a cutting from a wild rose to grow in their own gardens or to gather fresh leafy greens to use in a salad.

I'd done it several times myself, although it had been years since I'd hunted for morel mushrooms in the spring, back in Missouri. My parents had a knack for locating the sponge-like fungi, which my mom breaded and fried in butter with a little bit of olive oil. They were really yummy, I thought, with a touch of nostalgia for times past. Now that my parents were living in Florida, and I resided in Arizona, there'd be no more treks in the woods to hunt morels.

Susan told me that she hadn't made her statement yet, so I clued her in that now might be a good time to take care of it since Lieutenant Belmont was at his doctor's office.

"It'd be just my luck that he'd come back while I'm there, but I guess I might as well get it over with. I feel so depressed—first Natalie and then Eric. He was only forty-five. I know what a hard time he's had since Natalie died, but he should have had lots of years left, and they could have been good ones. Maybe he could have made a new life for himself. He acted almost like the old Eric when he came into the Roadrunner to see me the day of the Christmas parade. Whatever he wanted to show me, he felt excited about it. I can't wrap my head around the fact that he's gone. Chip was shocked when I told him. He and Josh have been friends since grade school. I have a feeling Josh is going to need his friends more than ever in the next few weeks. Eric was the only close family Josh had left, and now he's gone, too."

"Poor Josh. I can't imagine what he must be feeling," I said.

"And then to show up when the coroner and police were there: it was such a shock."

"It was terrible. I feel sorry for Kayla, too. Here, she thought she was doing Eric a favor by bringing him dessert from the fair."

"I know. She shouldn't blame herself." Susan sighed. "I guess I might as well get this over with. I'm keeping my fingers crossed that the lieutenant doesn't come back to work while I'm at the station."

Poor Susan. She'd never forget the trauma of her arrest. Lieutenant Belmont had never apologized to her for his mistake, either. No wonder she didn't want to see him.

After a stop at the supermarket, I headed home with a few supplies, including a new candy thermometer. My old one had let me down big time when I'd attempted to make penuche a few days earlier. I wanted to have some on hand because it was my dad's favorite, but because of the thermometer failure, I'd ended up with ingredients that I'd boiled until the so-called candy was as hard as a rock. I couldn't remove it from the pan, so I threw the whole unfortunate conglomeration in the garbage, pan and all. Needless to say, I was hoping for better results next time.

As usual, my affable retriever greeted me enthusiastically at the kitchen door. Mona Lisa decided she wanted to join the club, too, and she brushed against my ankle, meowing until I scooped her up in my arms. Satisfied after a brief moment, she leaped to the top of her kitty tree, where she could keep her eye on Laddie and me.

I put the groceries away, took Laddie outside for a game of fetch, then fixed a sandwich for lunch and distributed a couple of treats into Laddie's bowl. As soon as Mona Lisa saw my last maneuver, she jumped down, went straight to her bowl, and waited for her own treat. I obliged her, and she quickly swallowed it and returned to her perch, swatting at Laddie on the way. Luckily, he'd seen her coming and swung his head away before her paw connected with his nose.

Although I wasn't feeling especially inspired and I admitted I was sorely tempted to procrastinate, it really was time to get to work. I'd put a large landscape on hold while finishing Mr. Big's portrait. Before mixing oils on my palette, I secreted my painting of the little dog in the studio's closet, because Belle was very likely to pop by later.

I considered landscapes, painted in an expressionistic abstract manner, my signature style. By contrast, I painted pet portraits in a very realistic way, and my inclusion of them in my repertoire had definitely improved my bottom line, but my first love was the imaginative landscapes that weren't selling at the moment. For that matter, neither were the pet portraits. If someone commissioned their dog's or cat's picture now, I wouldn't have enough time to complete it before Christmas, so it was useless to hope that someone would order a last-minute pet portrait for a holiday gift.

Perhaps I should try to find more gallery representation. I thought, as I carefully layered paint on my fiery red-orange landscape, reflecting a blistering desert scene bathed in radiant sunlight. Many artists were represented by several galleries, each in a different city. Thus far, I was represented by the Roadrunner and the Crystal Star Gallery, back in Kansas City, where I'd had my one-and-only solo show.

The trek from Lonesome Valley to Phoenix or nearby Scottsdale took only an hour and a half. Since Scottsdale was well known nationwide for its many art galleries, and it was so close, maybe it was time to expand my horizons and seek representation from one of them.

The more I thought about it, the more I liked the idea. Although in the months since I'd moved to Lonesome Valley, I'd driven to Phoenix only a few times to pick up Emma or my parents at the Sky Harbor Airport and a couple of times to deliver a large painting to a specialist in shipping art, it was certainly close enough to make the prospect appealing, since I could personally deliver my artwork to a Scottsdale gallery and not have to worry about shipping it.

Emma would be arriving in a few days, so, since I'd be driving to Phoenix anyway, I could go early and explore a few galleries before her flight arrived at eight o'clock. I put my brush down to check the schedule she'd texted me and saw that she was coming in at eight in the morning, rather than in the evening, as I'd mistakenly recalled. That could work, too, though, if Emma didn't mind stopping for a leisurely breakfast before spending some time scouting around art galleries so that I could find out which ones might be good prospects for me to approach. I called Emma, and she loved the idea, especially since she planned on spending most of her semester break working at the feed store, so her holiday would be more work than vacation time. She'd worked there for Dennis in the summer, too, and liked having the extra spending money she earned.

With my plans to visit the galleries in Scottsdale settled, I returned to my landscape, only to be interrupted by a call. If I'd been really engrossed, I might have chosen to ignore it, but my curiosity won out. As soon as I picked up my cell phone, I saw that Susan was the caller. By now, she'd had ample time to visit the police station and make her statement. I really hoped she hadn't had the bad luck to run into Lieutenant Belmont there, as she'd feared.

"I just left the station," she said breathlessly, "and I found out why Eric thought his financial situation was about to improve and what it was he wanted to show me."

Chapter 12

"I'm all ears."

"Remember the paperwork we saw on Eric's desk?"

"Yes, it had a big black clip holding it together."

"That's right. It was a copy his lawyer gave him. He was suing the company that owned the helicopter that crashed, killing Natalie. I'm sure that was what Eric wanted to show me."

"How did you find out?'

"Dave Martinez showed me the paperwork and asked if I thought it might be what Eric intended to show me. I told him I thought it must be. Dave's such a nice guy. He made the whole giving-a-statement thing easy. I wasn't at the station very long, and Lieutenant Belmont never showed up, so I lucked out on that score."

"I'm a bit confused. Why did Eric wait two years before suing, I wonder."

"Well, I think I know the answer to that one. After the crash, Eric was pretty much in a state of shock for months. He was so depressed he probably couldn't get it together enough to consider suing. Like I told you before, the day of the Christmas parade, when he came into the gallery, was the first time since

Natalie died that Eric seemed like his old self. There's just one thing that puzzles me."

"What's that?"

"He acted as though all his financial problems would go away soon, but I can't imagine that a lawsuit would be resolved so quickly."

"Maybe his lawyer had negotiated a settlement."

"That must be it. Otherwise, if the case had gone to court, it could have dragged on and on. And there's no way of telling how it would be resolved."

After Susan and I finished our conversation, I worked on my landscape for a while longer. As I finished for the day and slipped my palette into the freezer to preserve the colors I'd mixed, it occurred to me that something was off. Our theory that a settlement in Eric's lawsuit was imminent didn't make sense unless he'd been a major con artist. Although a few people had characterized him as a poor businessman, nobody had called him a crook. Yet he'd filed for Chapter 7 bankruptcy protection. Surely, proceeds of any settlement he would receive in a lawsuit would be assets that he should have planned to use to pay his debts. Before their fight in the restaurant parking lot, he had promised his former partner that he would pay him everything he owed, but Eric had refused to make it official. I had no idea how his sudden death might affect those lingering legal issues. That would be one for lawyers to figure out.

Later in the afternoon, when Belle came over, I relived discovering Eric's body and told her about the carrot bar Susan and I had spotted on the counter of his kitchen island.

"Oh, that's terrible! Dennis and I had only heard about the three people who got sick at the fair. I haven't checked the news or turned on the radio since we came home. Have they ever figured out how it happened?"

"Not exactly. The health department took the carrot bars that were at the Pioneers' booth to be tested. Oh, I just remembered: the police chief's going to make a statement. It's just about time for the early news now. Let's check it out."

I aimed my remote toward the TV, turned it on, and selected the local news channel. What seemed like an endless number of ads ran before the announcer, his face set in a sober expression, came on with the first major story of the day.

A Lonesome Valley man is the latest victim of a rash of food poisonings traced to cookie bars sold at the high school's annual crafts fair on Saturday, when three people were hospitalized. They are due to be released from the hospital tomorrow, but Eric Thompson, a prominent Lonesome Valley businessman, wasn't so fortunate: he was pronounced dead Sunday evening, after neighbors found him unconscious and could not revive him.

The report was fairly accurate, although it became a bit muddled at the end, before cutting to a scene from the police chief's press conference. Standing outside the station with Dave Martinez and Lieutenant Belmont behind him, the chief stepped up to a microphone to announce that the type of poison which sickened the people at the high school and killed Eric had been identified. He then turned the microphone over to a health department official, who revealed that hemlock caused the food poisoning. He explained that the plant grows in Arizona, and all parts of the plant were poisonous.

A few reporters shouted questions, but the chief took over the mic and asked them to hold their questions until he completed his statement. He proceeded to ask the public to help, if anyone had information regarding the poisoned carrot bars, and gave a number of a hotline to call. The man from the health department reiterated a warning not to eat any carrot bars purchased at the fair.

I noticed that the chief hadn't said that the carrot bars had come from the Pioneers' booth, and I wondered whether that was a deliberate strategy on his part. Rebecca, at least, would be grateful that he hadn't mentioned the choir's booth as the source of the poisoned carrot bars.

After the warning, the chief called for questions, and he was immediately bombarded with inquiries about whether the poisoning had been accidental or deliberate.

"That's the million-dollar question," he said. "Either somebody innocently decided to use part of a hemlock plant in baking, or there's an evil individual out there who doesn't care about human life, somebody with a twisted mind who gets a sick thrill out of hurting other people."

The chief paused for a couple seconds and then looked straight at the camera.

"If that's the case, and you're watching me now, I'm putting you on notice: you won't get away with it."

Chapter 13

Sergeant Martinez and Lieutenant Belmont exchanged an uneasy glance at the chief's declaration, probably because they knew how difficult it would be to keep the chief's promise.

"Wow!" Belle exclaimed. "He didn't mince words, did he? If I were the clueless person who made the carrot bars, I'd probably be afraid to admit it after hearing that."

"I think you're right," I agreed. "I'm kind of surprised he was so vehement. I've met him a couple of times, and he always seemed very cool-headed."

"The accidental poisoning theory seems more plausible to me."

"I would believe that, too, except for the fact that Rebecca can't pin down where those carrot bars came from," I said. "Nobody has admitted to making them."

"Probably too scared to own up to it, especially now that a man's dead."

"If that's the case, whoever did it must be feeling very guilty."

Laddie interrupted our serious talk by nuzzling Belle's arm and putting his paw on her knee. She petted him and assured him that he'd see Mr. Big tomorrow.

"You hit the nail on the head, Belle. That's exactly what

Laddie wants. He hasn't seen his little buddy for a couple of days, and he misses him."

"Let's take them for a walk in the morning," Belle said. "I'll even get up early. Not as early as you, of course, but early for me. How about eight?"

"Good. That'll work. Tomorrow's my turn at the gallery, but I'm scheduled in the afternoon, so I don't have to be there until one."

"Eight it is, then. I'd better get home now and get organized. We were only gone for a day, but I feel like it was longer. See you in the morning."

After Belle went home, Laddie, Mona Lisa, and I spent a quiet evening in front of the television. While my pets snuggled close to me, one on each side, I watched a lighthearted holiday movie and tried not to think of the events of the past couple days. Putting them out of my mind proved an impossible task, though, and later that night I woke several times, only to drift back into a restless sleep again.

In the morning, after the bad night I'd had, I was more than happy to get out of bed when Laddie began tapping on my arm with his paw.

My golden boy pranced around, eager to go for a walk, but we'd have to wait for Belle and Mr. Big, and he settled for a romp in the backyard, followed by breakfast.

It was quarter after eight when Laddie's ears perked up and he raced to the kitchen door, whipping his feathery tail back and forth. As soon as I opened the door, Mr. Big ran in, tugging at his leash, and the two dogs greeted each other as though they'd been separated for months. I pulled on my parka, gloves, and a knit hat, and we were off.

Although the air was cold and crisp, the Arizona sun shone

brightly in a cloudless sky, and the day held the promise of warmer temperatures later on. It wasn't unusual for there to be a twenty-five or thirty-degree difference in temperature between the daily high and low.

"I thought maybe Rebecca and Greg would be in the park this morning," Belle said, "but I don't see them."

I looked around and spotted their neighbor across the street, coming out of his house with his two children, each sporting a backpack.

"Look! There's Carmen's husband Lew. He must be taking the kids to school."

I waved, but he wasn't looking toward the park, and he didn't see me. He and the children piled into his white painter's van and departed. Shortly after they left, Rebecca and Greg came out of their house with Skippy and Tucker, and we met them at the corner. The four dogs bounced around each other, snarling their leashes. After they settled down, we untangled their leashes and told them to sit. Laddie promptly complied, but Mr. Big and the terriers continued to wiggle until Greg raised his voice and commanded them to sit for a second time. Even Mr. Big paid attention, and Belle commended Greg for his success.

"I'm afraid Mr. Big's so rambunctious and easily distracted that he doesn't pay any attention to what I tell him half the time," she confessed.

"He seems fine now," I assured her.

"I happened to notice you coming toward the park," Rebecca said, "and I wanted to talk to you, but we waited until Lew left for school with the kids. Truth be told, I'm embarrassed to see him after what happened. I hope he and Carmen don't blame me."

"I'm sure they don't," I said. "You couldn't have known what was going to happen."

"No, but those carrot bars came from the Pioneers' booth, and now Greg's cousin Eric has died, too! I can't understand it. Nobody admits to making them. I've been over and over the list of baked goods and candy that our members made, and the decorated carrot bars are definitely not there."

"Maybe somebody delivered them to the wrong table," Belle suggested. "Once in a while, our library auxiliary members have other people drop off items for them."

"I suppose that could have happened," Rebecca said. "It certainly would explain why our members all deny having made them."

"If you ask me, the chief of police thinks it was deliberate by some weirdo with evil intentions, and I'm starting to think the same thing myself," Greg said. "It's very busy and crowded at the fair, during the last hour, especially. Anybody could have slipped those carrot bars into inventory without Rebecca or the other choir members who were working at our booth noticing."

"That's true. There were three of us working there, and we were really slammed. I know people were waiting in line."

"An accidental poisoning is bad enough," I said, "but a deliberate one is pure evil. Let's hope the police solve this soon."

"Hear, hear," Greg said. "Eric didn't deserve to die just because he loved anything sweet. We may have had our differences, but he was still family."

"Lonesome Valley used to be such a peaceful town," Rebecca lamented, as we began moving toward the path. The dogs jumped up, eager to continue their walk, and we all circled the park before Belle and I bid the Winterses goodbye.

Belle offered to host Laddie during my afternoon shift at the

Roadrunner, and I accepted her offer, knowing that Laddie would be happier playing with his little buddy than staying home alone with Mona Lisa.

The doggie playdate settled, I puttered around the house without accomplishing much until it was time to get ready to go to the gallery.

As I drove to Main Street, I allowed myself to fantasize that I'd sell a half-dozen pricey paintings there today, although I knew the reality would more likely be that I would sell nothing. At the fair, I'd told Susan and Chip that I hadn't sold a painting at the Roadrunner in three weeks. Now, a few days later, it was going on a month since I'd had a sale there, and I wasn't very likely to sell anything on a Tuesday.

The gallery was always busiest on the weekends, and our revenue tended to be the highest then, too. That didn't mean it wasn't worthwhile for the gallery to be open on weekdays, but traffic was certainly slower then. Perhaps today might be an exception, though, since quite a few holiday shoppers were bustling about downtown. It was the first Tuesday ever that I wasn't able to park near the gallery. Instead, I had to find a spot in the downtown parking lot and walk a few blocks to the Roadrunner.

"Hi, Dorothy," I said, as I walked into the gallery on the dot of one o'clock. "It's a good thing I left home early. I had to park in the lot, instead of out front."

Dorothy was Dawn Martinez's mother, and the two women owned a pottery studio, where they taught classes as well as designed their own ceramic creations.

"No problem," Dorothy told me. "You're right on time, and Pamela's here, too. She's back in the office, but, if it gets busy, she'll pitch in."

I put my coat and purse away and signed in for my four-hour shift. Dorothy was showing me her latest ceramic creation, a huge elaborately decorated platter, when the gallery door opened and a group of shoppers trooped in. Pamela, who'd left her office door open, must have heard the voices, and she came out into the gallery to greet the visitors with us. Every woman in the group carried at least one large shopping bag, which meant some of them were very likely to spend some of their Christmas shopping cash in the Roadrunner.

I helped a grandmother find a print of a horse for her granddaughter while Dorothy showed some of the other women necklaces and earrings from our jewelry display and Pamela talked to others about the paintings that had attracted their attention. As usual, tiny Pamela was dressed in beige, and, as usual, I couldn't help thinking about the contrast between her fashion choices and the bright, vibrant, colorful art she painted. It was as though she wanted to fade into the background, but she wanted her lively, bold pictures to grab people's attention.

More customers dropped in, and we sold several items, including prints, jewelry, note cards, and even a small painting. One customer took a great interest in the highly decorated platter Dorothy had been showing me earlier. Although she left without purchasing it, Dorothy thought the woman might return later.

After an hour or so, the gallery had cleared out with the exception of a retired couple who were leisurely making the rounds and studying every painting on the walls.

Pamela joined Dorothy and me as we chatted about the progress we'd made in our Christmas shopping.

"I'm a little worried about our Christmas party Sunday

night," Pamela confided. "After what happened at the high school fair, I'm not sure people will want to chance eating pot luck."

"Oh, I'm sure that was accidental," Dorothy said. "And I haven't heard about any more food poisoning since that poor man died the other night. Besides, we know everybody who's coming, and none of them are members of the Pioneers."

"What do you think, Amanda?" Pamela asked.

I remembered how I'd felt when I thought I'd eaten one of the poisoned carrot bars. "I suppose I'd be a bit cautious, but, like Dorothy said, we know everybody, although . . . ." I hesitated.

"What is it, Amanda?" Dorothy prompted.

"If it wasn't an accident . . . ."

"I don't know. I heard the chief suggest that possibility, but it's hard to believe."

"So you don't think we should cancel?" Pamela asked.

"I don't," Dorothy insisted. "The members look forward to the party. If you need an official food tester, I'll volunteer."

We laughed at her suggestion, but I certainly understood Pamela's concern, and I had to admit that I felt a wee bit uneasy, too. I didn't have time to dwell on my concern, though, because Lonesome Valley's vivacious mayor popped into the gallery just then. She wore the same dramatic red velvet cape trimmed with white faux fur that she'd worn in the Christmas parade. I'd assumed the cape was strictly a holiday costume, but, evidently, I'd been wrong. Melinda's lips were as red as her cape, thanks to her expert application of lipstick, and, with her dark brown hair and creamy complexion, she looked quite dramatic in an old-fashioned Hollywood glam kind of way.

"Hello, Melinda," Pamela exchanged a quick hug and an air

kiss with the mayor. That bright red lipstick definitely would have left its mark if she had connected with Pamela's cheek, so it was a good thing that hadn't happened.

The mayor turned to Dorothy and me and apologized for not remembering our names. I'd met her in person only once before myself, so it was no wonder that she'd forgotten my name. I probably wouldn't have remembered hers, either, except for the fact that she appeared on the local news so often.

"I'm here to buy a painting for my den," our mayor announced, "and I need a big one. Maybe a landscape."

Chapter 14

Before I could say a word, Melinda looked past us to the wall where Ralph's Western landscapes hung. If Melinda wanted a realistic painting, she couldn't go wrong by choosing one of Ralph's. My heart sank as she looked at one large elaborately framed depiction of a lake with birch trees in the background.

"This would be perfect for Bob's office, and it solves my annual problem of what to get him for Christmas. Could I arrange for it to be delivered? I'd like to surprise him."

"Of course," Pamela said. "We'll take care of it." She quickly moved to put a discrete "sold" sign next to the painting.

"Now, for our den, I'm looking for something a little more—I don't know—uh, artsy, but not so abstract that it's unrecognizable."

Pamela nudged me.

I don't know why I didn't speak up right away. "Melinda, I have some paintings you might like to see," I volunteered. I led her around the divider wall to the back of the gallery, where my landscapes were displayed. I thought she looked interested, but I hoped I wasn't indulging in wishful thinking.

She spent several minutes looking at the paintings before pointing to one of the smaller ones. "I like the colors of this one, but it's way too small for my space," she said, gazing at a woodland scene in soft greens, blues, and shades of yellow. "Do you have anything larger in similar colors?"

"Yes, I do. It's in my studio. You're welcome to come by to see it, or I'd be happy to bring it to your house, so that you can see how it would look in your den."

Jolly strains of "Jingle Bells" burst forth, and Melinda reached into the folds of her velvet cape and came up with her cell phone. She stepped away from me and turned her back. From what little I could hear, the conversation concerned some official city business.

"I'm going to have to go now. Do you have a card?"

I reached into my pocket, produced one, and handed it to her. Knowing that she was leaving without making a commitment, I felt disappointed. The big sale I'd hoped for wasn't about to materialize.

"I'll call you to arrange the delivery of the painting to Bob's office," she said to Pamela, as she hastily headed for the door.

"You win some; you lose some," I muttered, after she left.

"If I were you, I wouldn't give up," Pamela advised, "Melinda's a good prospect. Maybe you could contact her later and suggest bringing the painting out to her ranch, where she can see how it looks in her den."

"Do you really think so?"

"Yes," Pamela and Dorothy said in unison.

"What do you have to lose?" Pamela asked.

"That's true. All right, it couldn't hurt to give it a try, I guess." I could have kicked myself for not being a bit more aggressive in my sales pitch. Typically, I stood back and let potential customers decide what they liked without pushing them too hard. I consoled myself that at least I'd had the presence of mind to suggest an in-home viewing. Even though I knew I'd never be super at sales, at least that had been a start in the right direction.

Pamela and Dorothy decided to take a look at the list of food that members had pledged to bring to our Christmas party, scheduled to be held in the Roadrunner's large classroom. While they put their heads together over the sign-up sheet, my mind wandered back to the poison carrot bars, and I wondered how the maker had managed to put hemlock in them.

"No carrot bars, I see," Pamela announced. "That's good."

I didn't remind her that if hemlock could be put in carrot bars without its being noticed by the person who was eating them, then it could possibly be used to poison all sorts of other food, too. A shiver went up my spine as I contemplated the possibility that the carrot bars at the high school holiday crafts fair had been poisoned deliberately. Then another thought occurred to me. Before I realized it, I'd said it out loud: "Where would someone find hemlock around here?"

"What's that?" Dorothy asked.

"Oh, sorry. I was just wondering if hemlock grows anyplace in Lonesome Valley."

"Hmm. I can't tell one plant from another myself," she said, "but I know someone who can. She used to teach botany and biology at the high school, but she's retired now."

"I bet you're talking about Sylvia Costa. I had her for biology in high school," Pamela said.

"Yes, so did Dawn. Mrs. Costa was Dawn's botany teacher, too. I remember she took the class on a couple of field trips."

"She sounds like an expert on the local flora. I wonder if she'd mind talking to me about it to satisfy my curiosity."

"I doubt she'd mind," Dorothy said. "She's been retired for

several years, but I think she's still pretty active. I saw her at the supermarket the other day. It looked like she was about to start her holiday baking big time."

"You don't happen to have her phone number, do you?"

"No, but I'll bet she has a landline."

"OK, I'll try directory assistance."

"No need," Pamela said. "We have a really old phone book on the top shelf of the bookcase in my office. Why don't you try that first? We'll hold the fort while you give her a call."

"Thanks. This shouldn't take long."

I walked down the hallway to Pamela's office and spotted the phone book right where she'd said it would be. Sylvia Costa's name was easy to find. She was the only Costa in the old phone book. I ran my finger across the line of tiny print, which listed her address as well as her phone number.

The street name sounded familiar, but why? At first, I couldn't place it, but then it came to me.

Eric Thompson had lived on Copper Valley Road. Quickly, I flipped the pages, hoping to find a listing for the Thompsons. Sure enough; there was one. They had a landline, too. At least, they'd had one twelve years ago, but it wasn't their phone number that caught my attention. It was their house number—792. It, also, had sounded familiar, but I couldn't remember it for sure. Sylvia Costa's house number was listed as 794. She was Eric's next-door neighbor.

Chapter 15

The very same next-door neighbor Brian's nephew Josh had called a "witch" knew all about local plants and enjoyed baking, to boot. I wondered why Josh had yelled only at Mrs. Costa but ignored all the other neighbors the night his uncle had died. Before I called Mrs. Costa from the landline in Pamela's office, I speculated about what that might mean. When she answered, I immediately mentioned that Dorothy and Pamela had recommended her as an expert on local plants before inquiring whether she'd mind satisfying my curiosity about hemlock that grew in Arizona.

"I'm a little confused," she said. "What's your interest in all this? Are you working with the police?"

"Just curious," I told her. "My friend and I were the ones who called for help for Eric Sunday night, and we were at the high school crafts fair, too. We'd been working in the Roadrunner's booth in the afternoon, and we saw the ambulances arriving as we left. I'm not working in any official capacity."

"You say you know Dorothy and Pamela?"

"Yes. We're all members of the Roadrunner Gallery. I'm calling you from the gallery, as a matter of fact."

"Well, all right. I'd like to speak to Dorothy for a moment, if you don't mind."

"I'll go get her. I'm in the office, and she's out front," I explained hastily. I put the receiver down on Pamela's desk and went to tell Dorothy that Mrs. Costa wanted to speak with her. Although a few browsers had come into the Roadrunner, Pamela was assisting them, so Dorothy was free.

"Oh, I bet I know what she wants," Dorothy said, as we walked back to the office. "I offered to lend her one of my old cookbooks that I put together for a fundraiser years ago for the high school PTA. When I saw her the other day, we got to talking about some of the recipes that were in it that we just never seem to hear about anymore. They're good recipes, but maybe they're out of fashion now. Anyway, she wants to make some of them for the holidays."

It turned out that Sylvia Costa did indeed want to borrow Dorothy's old cookbook, but she also wanted to make sure that I really knew Dorothy. After Dorothy vouched for me, she told Sylvia she'd drop the cookbook off to her later and handed the phone back to me.

"How about tomorrow at ten at my place?" she suggested.

"Thank you, Mrs. Costa. I appreciate it. I'll see you then."

After I hung up, I wondered if I'd gone too far. After all, the police were investigating the poisonings, and I was no detective. But then again, it couldn't hurt to gain a little knowledge, I thought. Aware that I was deliberately procrastinating, arranging to talk to Sylvia Costa when I probably should have been more concerned with contacting the mayor in an effort to revive her interest in my landscape, I returned to the gallery and processed several sales before closing time rolled around.

We all left the Roadrunner a little after five, going our separate ways to our cars. Quite a few shoppers headed in the same direction I was going, toward the downtown parking lot. It was dark by this time, but the street lamps on Main Street provided plenty of light. The Downtown Merchants' Association had decorated the lamp posts with greenery and huge red bows, and most of the merchants' holiday window displays featured twinkling Christmas lights, adding to the festive mood of the shoppers.

When I backed out of my parking spot in the downtown lot, I came within inches of being clobbered by a large van that had whipped around the corner going way faster than any driver should in a crowded lot. I slammed on my brakes, just in the nick of time, and the van's driver sped away, oblivious to the near miss.

Having avoided a potential accident, I was happy to arrive home, none the worse for wear. I pulled into my carport and trekked across Belle's front yard to her door, where Laddie waited for me on the other side. When I stopped to give him a hug, Mr. Big, not wanting to be left out, squeezed his way in for a snuggle, too.

"How'd it go at the gallery today?" Belle asked. She knew I'd been concerned with my finances of late.

"Oh, the usual. We had some sales, but I didn't sell any of my own paintings. I came close, though." I told Belle about the mayor's interest in one of my landscapes and that we'd been interrupted, after which she'd had to leave before she'd made a commitment.

"That sounds like a good opportunity," Belle enthused. "You can't afford to pass it up."

"I know I should contact her. I'm just not sure what the best approach would be. I don't want to come across as too aggressive."

"There's no way that's going to happen. You said the large landscape with the colors she wants is in your studio, right?"

I nodded.

"Why don't you send her a personal invitation to attend your Friday open studio, along with a note reminding her that the landscape she's interested in will be on display?"

"That's a good idea. Should I email it?"

"She probably gets a ton of email, and it's far too easy to ignore. I think it's worth delivering a handwritten invitation to her office."

"OK, I'll do it. You really think it might work?"

"You never know, but it can't hurt to try. If she's really interested, she might show up. If she doesn't, you can always call her later."

"Sounds like a plan."

Later that evening, I rummaged through my packets of note cards featuring my artwork printed on them that I sold during studio tours. I didn't make a lot of money from them, but they sold consistently, and people often liked to make a small purchase during Friday night studio tours.

Finally, I found the card I was looking for. Printed on the front was the image of the painting I hoped to sell the mayor. I sat down at my desk and wrote an invitation to her to drop by during tour hours Friday, adding that I could show her the painting another time if it would be more convenient. I took pains to write neatly and legibly, since I had a tendency to scrawl. Satisfied, I slipped the card into its envelope, wrote the mayor's name on the front, dribbled some blue sealing wax on the tip of the flap, and pressed my seal of an artist's palette into the wax. Satisfied that I'd made a crisp impression with my seal, I left the envelope on my desk to retrieve the following morning before I left to meet Mrs. Costa. I figured I could drop the invitation off at the mayor's office in Lonesome Valley's city hall on my way.

The following morning, I left the house in plenty of time to stop by the city hall before meeting with Mrs. Costa. Since she hadn't seemed especially eager to see me, I didn't want to upset her by showing up late, but when I walked into the mayor's reception room, her assistant wasn't there. The door to the mayor's office stood wide open, and I could see that Melinda wasn't there, either. Ordinarily, I would have waited, but since I had no idea how long it might be, I placed the invitation front and center on the assistant's desk. As I turned to leave, a young woman came in through a side door and sat down behind the desk.

"Hi, I'm Cassie, the mayor's assistant. May I help you?"

"I just dropped off an invitation for the mayor. It's right there," I said, indicating the envelope I'd placed on the desk.

"I'll see that she gets it," she promised.

My errand accomplished, I drove to Copper Valley Road and parked in front of Mrs. Costa's house. Before I went to the door, I called the mayor's office to make sure my invitation had been delivered, but my call went to voicemail, and I opted to try again later, rather than leaving a message. As I got out of my SUV, I glanced at the house and saw a curtain dropping back into place. Mrs. Costa must have been looking out for me. When she opened the door while I was still climbing the steps, I knew I'd been right. It was the same maneuver that had upset Josh when he'd arrived at Eric's house, only to find police cars with flashing lights and neighbors gawking at the officers' activity.

"Amanda?"

"Yes, I'm Amanda, Mrs. Costa. Nice to meet you."

"Call me Sylvia, dear," she said, as she stepped aside. "Come in."

I stepped into her living room, which looked like it hadn't been redecorated in decades. Worn beige shag carpet covered the floor, and a sofa and chair sported a matching, oversize brown plaid pattern that had once been popular. The coffee table was covered with knickknacks and stacks of books. There were so many pillows on the sofa that, at first, I didn't see the black cat nestled among them, and I was startled when it leaped down from the sofa and scampered off, disappearing behind a bookcase.

Although I'd never believed the superstition that a black cat crossing someone's path brought bad luck, I couldn't help thinking about it when Sylvia's cat ran across mine.

"What's your kitty's name?" I asked.

"That's Midnight, but I call her Middie for short. She's skittish around strangers. She'll probably hide for a while."

"I have a cat, too. Mona Lisa's her name. She has all sorts of hiding spots."

Sylvia smiled and led me through the living room to the kitchen in the back of the house. Scents of vanilla and cinnamon filled the air, and the countertops were filled with gift plates of cookies and candy done up in red cellophane and tied with green ribbon. The oven timer dinged as we came into the room, and Sylvia took a pair of potholders, reached into the oven, and pulled out a cookie sheet. She set it aside so that the cookies could cool and turned off the oven.

"Have a seat, Amanda. Let's have some coffee."

I slid into the bench seat in her kitchen alcove, where a ceramic snowman decorated the table before me.

"Milk or sugar?"

"Black is fine. Thanks."

She put a mug of coffee and a napkin in front of me and a

plate of cookies in the center of the table before pouring her own coffee and returning to sit opposite me. She took a cookie and set it on her napkin and slid the plate toward me. "Help yourself. I make these only at Christmas."

I nibbled the treat. "Mmm. It's very good."

"The neighbors seem to like them."

"Are those all for your neighbors?" I asked, nodding toward the red-wrapped plates of goodies on the counter.

"Yes, for everybody on the block and a few friends."

"That's a big job."

"I'll say. I spent all day yesterday making candy. Today, it's the cookies, but I'm all done now. That's the last batch I just took out of the oven. But you didn't come to hear about my holiday baking. Tell me, what would you like to know?"

"Well, as I told you on the phone yesterday, I'm curious. I've never heard of anyone who's been poisoned by hemlock before, except for Socrates, of course. Is there a lot of it growing around here?"

"Not a lot, but I've seen it in the county, mostly up around Miners' Creek. It needs some moisture, more than some of our desert plants. You're not too likely to find it in someone's backyard here in town. Do you know what the plant looks like?"

"Yes, I found some pictures of it online and read about a few instances of people who ate the root, thinking it was some kind of carrot."

"Fools," she said, startling me with her vehemence. "Some people take it into their heads that anything natural is safe. That's far from the truth. Ingesting part of a plant discovered in the wild when you don't know what it is can lead to trouble, as happened in the cases you read about."

"How much hemlock would it take to kill a person?"

"No studies have been done on that, as far as I know, but obviously not a lot, or Eric would still be alive."

"My friend Susan told me Eric and his wife had lived in the house next door for several years."

"Yes. Natalie inherited the house after her great-grandmother died. I always got along quite well with Natalie. Unfortunately, I can't say the same for Eric."

"Oh?"

"He was always covering for his nephew Josh. Josh was one of my students, and I can tell you this: that boy's trouble with a capital 'T.'"

Chapter 16

"I noticed he was quite upset when he found out about his uncle, but isn't that only natural? It came as a shock."

"I wasn't referring to that."

Neither of us mentioned that he'd called Sylvia a "witch" at the time.

"No. It goes back to high school and his lack of character, even then."

"What do you mean?"

"It's a long story, but the short version is Josh cheated on a biology test, and I caught him red-handed. The penalty, besides getting a zero on the test, of course, was supposed to be automatic suspension from the basketball team, but the coach convinced the principal to let Josh serve detention, rather than suspending him from the team. After that, Josh found all kinds of nasty ways to get back at me, like letting the air out of my tires, but I could never prove it, so he got away with it. I tried to talk to Eric, but he believed Josh could do no wrong."

"I'm sorry that happened to you," I said sincerely, wondering whether Josh had mended his ways or perhaps Sylvia had exaggerated the incident.

"To tell you the truth, I'm really hoping Josh decides to sell the house, rather than move in. I'd hate to have him for a next-door neighbor."

"He's Eric's heir?"

"I assume so."

Sylvia probably didn't know about Eric's precarious financial situation, but if it had been as bad as I thought, chances were good that Josh wouldn't have much choice but to put his uncle's house on the market.

Sylvia insisted on giving me one of her gift-wrapped plates of goodies before I left. When I protested that I didn't want to leave her short, she told me she always made a few extras.

I thanked her for the treats, and as we headed for the front door, Middie peeked out from her hiding place behind the bookcase. Suddenly, she decided to return to her nest on the sofa, and she shot back across the room so quickly that I almost tripped over her as she crossed my path for the second time that day.

"Stay put now, Middie," Sylvia said mildly, as she opened the front door for me.

After I walked down the steps, I turned to wave and saw Sylvia at the window. She waved back, and then the curtain dropped.

I kept a box in the back of my SUV to corral groceries so the bags wouldn't slide around while I was driving. I put Sylvia's gift in it and closed the hatch. I was about to get into the car when the couple who'd tried to help Susan and me the night Eric died approached.

"Hi," the man said. "Are you helping Josh clear out the place?"

"No. I was just here to see Mrs. Costa."

"I'm sorry. I don't think we ever introduced ourselves the

other night," his wife said. "I'm Rachel; this is my husband Jack, and our dog's name is Charlie." Charlie wagged his tail and sniffed my feet.

"Amanda Trent," I said, stooping to pet the little beagle.

"They say she's a witch, you know," Jack said.

"Jack, that's crazy talk," his wife said. "Mrs. Costa's a perfectly nice old lady."

"Eric and Josh didn't seem to think so. I heard Eric yelling at her just last week. She was outside on her porch, and as soon as she heard him, she went inside and slammed the door. Later, I saw her peering out from behind the curtain, and she was holding that black cat of hers. She does that all the time. It's spooky."

"Don't be ridiculous, Jack. If someone was yelling at me, I'd go inside, too. As far as her looking out from behind the curtain, she probably wants to see what's going on in the neighborhood. She's not the only one. Remember how many people were watching the other night?"

"Yeah, I suppose, but you have to admit she looks witchy with her scraggly gray hair and black clothing. She's always carrying around her black cat, and her broom's right there on the front porch."

"Because she uses it to sweep the porch, silly. You've watched one too many Halloween movies."

"Woo-oo-oo!" Jack managed to make the word reverberate in an eerie way, and Charlie howled at the weird sound.

"I think that's our signal to get going," Rachel said. "Bye now."

The couple ambled down the street while Charlie tugged at his leash in an effort to hurry them along, I suspected.

Although Jack had sounded almost serious when he'd

mentioned that people thought Mrs. Costa was a witch, I definitely had the impression that he'd been teasing his wife.

I drove home thinking that I hadn't learned too much about hemlock, but now I knew that Eric and his neighbor had been at odds. Had their dispute been so serious that Sylvia Costa had poisoned Eric? She knew where to find hemlock, and she certainly knew how to bake. Nobody at the craft fair would have suspected a thing amiss if she'd brought some carrot bars in and slipped them onto the table at the Pioneers' booth. But if she had, that would mean she didn't mind poisoning other people in an effort to poison her neighbor. And there would have been no way she could have controlled whether Eric got any carrot bars, even if she knew he enjoyed such treats, unless she put them in his kitchen herself. All those actions would have been devious, and Sylvia didn't strike me as a devious person.

Then, again, she had the habit of surreptitiously watching her neighbors. Maybe she knew more than anyone realized.

Chapter 17

I wondered whether the police had questioned her, and I thought perhaps I should put a bug in Dave Martinez's ear. Sylvia might have seen something significant from behind her curtains, and she might not even realize it.

When I arrived home, I put speculation out of my mind as I treated Mona Lisa and Laddie to a mid-day snack, followed by playtime, a game of catch in the backyard for Laddie and a round of chasing her feather toy for Mona Lisa. The day had turned overcast and gray, and the temperature had dropped considerably. It would have been a good time to curl up beside a cozy fire, but I had no fireplace, so that wasn't going to happen. The gloomy day affected us all, and soon Mona Lisa and Laddie were both napping while I lay down on the sofa with a yawn and drifted off to sleep.

It couldn't have been more than a minute or two before I heard my phone ringing. I hadn't intended to take a nap, but only to rest for a moment. I jumped up and retrieved my cell phone from the kitchen counter. I didn't recognize the number, but that would never prevent me from answering because there was always the possibility that a potential customer who was interested in my artwork could be calling.

In hopes that was the case, I answered by stating my name.

"This is Cassie Lindell from the mayor's office. Mrs. Gibbs asked me to let you know that she'll stop by your studio Friday evening if she can find the time. It's been a terribly busy week."

"Thanks so much for letting me know." If I sold Melinda the painting Friday night, I wouldn't have to worry about paying my bills for the next couple of months.

"I think I'll drop by myself," Cassie said. "I haven't ever been to any of the local studios, and I keep hearing about the tour. Have you been a stop on it long?"

"I joined the tour in March."

"Perfect. I'm looking forward to seeing your artwork. I loved the landscape on your card, and your painter's palette seal was so cute." I could hear voices in the background, so it came as no surprise when Cassie said she'd better get back to work.

Psyched as I felt, I couldn't wait to tell Belle the good news. I called her and asked her over for coffee. While I brewed a nice blend of French roast that Belle liked, I removed the red cellophane from the plate of cookies Sylvia had given me and set it, along with some napkins, on my little dining table. I planned to have coffee, too, instead of my usual tea. Some caffeine might help me shake my drowsiness.

When Belle came to the door with Mr. Big, Laddie snoozed right through her distinctive tapping, but he woke up when Mr. Big pounced on his tail. The two dogs ran around my tiny living room until I called a halt, and they both sat politely, while I rewarded them each with a baby carrot, a whole one for Laddie and half for Mr. Big. After they ate their carrots, they settled down, side by side, on the floor to watch Belle and me. I'm sure they wouldn't have minded sampling the butterscotch shortbread cookies, which had been dipped in chocolate, but since eating chocolate was a big no-no for dogs, I didn't feel a bit tempted to offer them any.

"First Greg, then you," Belle said, looking at Mr Big. "Why is it he behaves for everyone but me?"

"Well, I kind of bribed him with the carrot, so I'm not sure that counts."

Laddie and Mr. Big continued to keep a watchful eye on Belle and me while we munched our cookies and I brought her up to date on my visit with Sylvia Costa and the mayor's response to my card. As soon as they figured out that no more snacks would be forthcoming, Laddie and Mr. Big dropped their chins to the floor, and before long, they both fell fast asleep.

"Mr. Big isn't usually so quiet," Belle observed. "I hope he's feeling all right."

"I think the weather may have gotten to him. Laddie and Mona Lisa both act tired, and I almost went to sleep earlier, too."

"I hope that's all it is. If he doesn't perk up by tomorrow, I think I'll take him to the vet for a check-up."

"That reminds me. Laddie has an appointment with the vet this week. I almost forgot about it." I grabbed my purse, which I'd left sitting on the kitchen counter, took out my wallet, and found the appointment card. "Oh, good; it's not until Friday. For a minute, I was afraid it might have been today."

"I bet you get a reminder call from the office staff sometime tomorrow."

"That's true. I guess I didn't need to worry about forgetting. I've been so distracted the last few days."

"No wonder, what with the poisonings and you and Susan finding Eric's body. I know you're worried about money, too, but I have a good feeling about that landscape the mayor's interested in. I bet she buys it when she comes to your studio Friday night."

"I sure hope so. That's *if* she comes. Her assistant emphasized that Melinda's really busy this week."

"If she weren't interested, she probably wouldn't have responded to your note. I think that's a good sign."

"Fingers crossed."

"On another subject, have you heard from Brian lately?"

"Not since before the poisonings. He's going to be shocked when I tell him what happened."

We chatted for a while longer before Belle cajoled a reluctant Mr. Big to come home with her. I spent the rest of the afternoon doing a few chores before I settled down with a book I'd been intending to read while Laddie napped at my feet and Mona Lisa snoozed on the wide arm of my chair.

Coincidentally, Brian called me that very evening. My drowsy pets didn't stir when the phone rang. I hoped we'd all feel peppier in the morning.

Brian listened without saying much when I told him about the events of the past few days.

"Amanda, promise me you'll be careful," he said. "It doesn't sound as though the police have a handle on what's going on there. Some psycho could be behind the poisonings."

"Yes, I know. It's a scary thought."

"Probably best not to eat anything you haven't prepared yourself until the cops find out where that poison came from."

"I suppose so," I said, thinking of the plate of goodies Sylvia had given me, but since I'd already eaten a few of the cookies with no ill effects, and I'd seen Sylvia eat one herself, I wasn't worried. "I wish I had better news to tell you, but I thought you'd want to know what's going on in town."

"I do. So much for thinking I moved to a quiet little town. I have some good news, though. At least, potentially good news."

"You're getting a promotion?" I guessed.

"No, not exactly, but close. A headhunter contacted me to ask if I'd be interested in another job. When he told me about it, I said I was."

My heart sank. Brian worked as a manager on an oil rig in the Gulf of Mexico, but I knew there were plenty of rigs on the other side of the world, and I doubted he'd be flying home every month if he worked on one of them. "What is it?" I asked.

"Something a little different from what I've been doing, and it's actually in Southern Arizona, maybe about a three- or four-hour drive from Lonesome Valley, but that's closer to home than I am now. I could come home every weekend if I get the job. Other people will be interviewing, so it's not a sure thing, but I'm kind of excited about the idea of managing a new solar power plant. I've always thought that, with all the sunshine in Arizona, we should be harnessing that energy."

"That sounds great. Do you have an interview scheduled yet?"

"Yep, just a few days after I get back, the first week in January. I'm trying not to count on it too much, though."

"I doubt the recruiter would have contacted you if you weren't a top candidate. I bet you have a good shot at it. I can tell by the way you spoke about solar energy that you're enthusiastic about it. That goes a long way, I think."

As we moved on to less weighty topics, I kept thinking about the prospect of Brian's changing jobs. I could tell it meant a lot to him, and I hoped he'd be the one chosen to manage the solar facility. If so, we'd see each other more frequently. I wondered how a new schedule would affect our budding romance, but only time would tell.

Chapter 18

Even though I hadn't sold any paintings lately, I still needed to keep up production, and I hadn't been doing a very good job of it lately. With nothing on my schedule for Thursday, I planned to spend the entire day in my studio painting, so after a brisk morning walk with Laddie and a quick breakfast, I went to work.

Despite my habit of procrastinating, I'd managed to produce enough work to display in my studio for tour visitors as well as fill my allotted fifteen-linear-feet space in the Roadrunner and send a few canvasses to the Crystal Star Gallery in Kansas City, where I had a small following. If I succeeded in gaining representation at one of the galleries in Scottsdale, I'd have to accelerate my pace at least a little, especially considering the occasional commission I received for a pet portrait.

By two o'clock in the afternoon, I was congratulating myself for making good progress. I'd worked steadily, taking only a few short breaks. I squeezed a dab of viridian green from its tube onto my palette and began mixing it with some titanium white and cadmium yellow to get just the tint of olive green I wanted to apply to some of the foliage on my landscape. Sometimes, I mixed colors directly onto the canvas, but the detail work involved in painting the foliage made it more practical to mix this particular hue on my palette. I applied a bit of the mixture and stepped back to look at the landscape. I decided it was darker than I'd intended, so I added a bit more white to achieve the desired effect.

My concentration broke when I heard the insistent ring of my cell phone. I was tempted to ignore it, but, on the off chance that a potential customer might be calling, I answered it.

Pamela didn't waste any time asking me if I could come in to work in the gallery for the rest of the afternoon.

"I have the worst toothache ever," she told me, "and the receptionist at my dentist's office can work me in right away. Susan's here, but we're really busy, and I don't think she can handle it alone."

I suspected an abscess was the cause of Pamela's distress. I'd had one once myself, and it had been no picnic. She'd need some antibiotics, pronto, if that were the case.

"OK, I'll be there as soon as I can. It'll probably be about twenty minutes before I can get there."

"Thanks so much, Amanda. I owe you one."

Pamela had done me plenty of favors since I'd joined the Roadrunner, and I didn't think she owed me a thing. I assured her I was happy to help.

I hurriedly put my paints away, changed clothes, swiped on some lipstick, and bade Laddie goodbye. I didn't see Mona Lisa, who must have been lurking in one of her hiding places.

There were even more shoppers crowding downtown than there had been a couple of days earlier, and I had to park in the city lot again and walk a few blocks to the Roadrunner.

A line had formed at the counter, and Susan was working as fast as she could to process each transaction. With me bagging and

Susan ringing up each sale, the work went faster. The Roadrunner had only one register, so it could get hectic during busy times.

"Pamela already left for the dentist," Susan told me when the rush had subsided.

"I figured. I bet she has an abscess. I've had one before, and it was extremely painful, almost unbearable, really, but once I started on some antibiotics, it started to feel better."

"It sounds awful. I'm lucky. I've never had so much as a twinge," Susan told me. "Knock on wood," she said, as she tapped on the wooden countertop.

The tinkling of a bell caught my attention as the gallery door swung open. It was a new feature that hadn't been there when I'd worked on Tuesday.

Looking a bit startled by the bell, Chip came into the gallery. "What's with the bell, Aunt Susan?" he asked. "Something for the holidays?"

"I guess it's permanent," she informed him. "Rich installed it yesterday."

"Is he still giving Pamela grief over me?" Chip asked.

Unfortunately, Chip and Pamela had had a brief fling several months earlier, and Pamela's husband Rich suspected as much. To keep the peace, Chip had resigned from the Roadrunner's board, stopped using the apartment over the gallery as his studio, and scheduled himself to work in the gallery only when Pamela wouldn't be around.

"I haven't heard Pamela mention it lately," Susan said.

"Neither have I," I confirmed.

"That's good. I wouldn't have dropped in today except that I happened to see Pamela going into Dr. Crawley's office when I drove by. If she's not coming back this afternoon, I'll stay and give you a hand."

"Good," I agreed. "It looks like you're just in time."

Another crowd entered the gallery, and it was all the three of us could do to keep up with helping our customers and processing sales, especially since several more shoppers came in after the large group.

Later, when only a couple of browsers remained in the gallery, Chip told us that Josh had scheduled Eric's memorial service for Saturday afternoon at a local funeral parlor. I'd barely known Eric, so I wasn't sure about going, but Susan asked me to attend with her, and since we'd been the ones to discover his body and she wanted me with her, I decided to attend.

"Josh is really broken up over his uncle's death," Chip said. "To make matters worse, Josh had to ask a relative to pay for the funeral because he couldn't afford it himself, and Eric's estate doesn't amount to anything because he had so many debts."

"Maybe Josh can eventually recoup because of the lawsuit," I speculated.

Chip shrugged.

I probably shouldn't have mentioned it, but since the cat was out of the bag, I plunged ahead and explained what I'd heard.

"Lawsuits usually take a long time, according to Josh," Chip said. "Even if the estate receives a settlement, I'm guessing it could be years away."

"I suppose Josh will have to sell Eric's house, in that case," I said.

"He's already listed it with a real estate broker, but, according to the broker, it'll end up being a break-even sale at best. Evidently, Eric hadn't made any mortgage payments in months and foreclosure proceedings have already begun."

"I don't get it," Susan said. "Eric seemed to think that he had a big payday coming, and he expected it soon, but, from what Josh told you, there doesn't seem to be any money in the mix at all." Susan shook her head. "Maybe he was kidding himself."

"Or he thought a settlement of his lawsuit was imminent," I reminded her.

"It isn't," Chip offered. "Josh said the suit could drag on forever. That's if Eric's lawyer doesn't drop the case. He told Josh he'd taken it on contingency, and he wasn't sure he could continue to put the hours in that he'd need to prepare."

"That's odd," Susan said. "I wonder why he agreed to take the case in the first place."

Chip shrugged. "No clue. All I know is that Josh has a big job on his hands settling the estate, and he's not going to inherit a dime. It'll probably end up costing him money."

"How's Josh holding up?" Susan asked.

"About as well as he can, I guess. He's upset that the police haven't been able to figure out what happened. I sure hope they come up with the answer before Josh does because, if not, watch out. He's liable to try to take down the poisoner himself."

Chapter 19

"What do you mean, Chip?" Susan asked in alarm.

"Josh has a temper when he's riled, and he's definitely riled now, but maybe he's being overly dramatic. I keep telling him to let the police investigate, but he says they're taking too long. Yesterday, he got into it with the chief, and he had Josh escorted out of the station."

"I know he's upset, but that's not going to do anybody any good," Susan said.

"Yeah, I know. I tried talking to him, but he wasn't in a listening mood. So did Kayla, but she didn't have any better luck than I did. I can understand why he's angry, but arguing with the chief of police won't help matters."

"No, it won't," I agreed.

"He even suggested that Eric's neighbor, Mrs. Costa, might have made the poison carrot bars. I told him that was nonsense."

"Why would he suggest such a thing?" Susan asked.

"She was his biology teacher in high school, and they didn't get along. She tried to get him kicked off the basketball team, but his uncle intervened. He claims she had it in for both of them."

I didn't comment on Chip's last statement. He'd omitted the reason that Josh should have been banned from the team. I wondered whether Chip knew the whole story. I probably would have asked him then and there, but several more shoppers came into the gallery, and we were busy until after our official closing time. Since Chip had to be at work at five, he left a few minutes early, so by the time Susan and I were ready to close the gallery, he'd already departed.

Susan had parked in the city lot, too, so we walked together to the car park and arranged to meet at the funeral parlor Saturday afternoon for Eric's memorial service.

As I pulled onto Main Street, I felt briefly tempted to stop at the supermarket's deli, which sold delicious homemade lasagna, but when I saw the number of vehicles in front of the store, I decided against it. Reheated leftovers would have to do. I'd been on my feet all day, and I was looking forward to relaxing, which is exactly what I did after I served my eager pets their dinner and ate my own.

After dinner, Mona Lisa wasn't content to sit on the arm of my chair. She plopped herself down in my lap and curled up, purring loudly. Laddie sat next to me, and I petted him while I watched an action movie on the TV. I raised the footrest on the chair and lowered the adjustable back a bit, and before I knew it, I fell asleep. I woke up in time to see the last minute of the movie. Of course, I had no idea what the story line was, so the wrap-up didn't mean much to me. After staying awake long enough to watch a silly reality show, I gave up for the night, and we all trooped off to bed.

Laddie's appointment at the vet's office the next morning was scheduled for nine o'clock, giving us plenty of time for a walk first. As soon as we got home, I took Laddie out to the patio and brushed his long coat thoroughly. He cooperated nicely, enjoying the grooming. After I finished, he pranced around me proudly.

"There, now," I told him. "You look very handsome for your doctor's appointment."

He wagged his tail as he accompanied me to the car and jumped into the back seat. Luckily, I had no trepidation about Laddie's upcoming visit with the vet since he'd always been a cooperative patient. Today, he was scheduled for his rabies booster shot. I'd transferred his records from our vet in Kansas City when we first moved to Lonesome Valley, and he'd had a checkup at the time. He hadn't been back to the vet since then, but I couldn't say the same for Mona Lisa, who'd had an ear infection and an upset tummy a few months later. Getting her into her kitty carrier had been an ordeal each time. On the last couple trips to the vet, I'd had to enlist help from both Belle and Dennis.

There'd been no such problems with my golden boy, though. Laddie hopped right out of the car when we arrived and made friends with a cocker spaniel while we waited in the reception room. After about ten minutes, a vet tech in a white coat called us back to the exam room.

"Dr. Madison will be right with you," the vet tech told me, placing a tray with a vial and a syringe on the countertop beside her before leaving Laddie and me to wait for the vet.

I sat down on the cushioned bench provided for pet parents, and Laddie stationed himself beside me.

When the door opened, my face must have registered my surprise. Dr. Madison, Laddie's vet, was a vivacious, curly-haired woman in her late thirties. The bald man who came into the room looked about sixty.

"You must have been expecting to see my daughter today."

"Yes, I didn't realize it was a family practice." The clinic's name—Lonesome Valley Veterinary Clinic—had given me no clue. For some reason, I had assumed that the younger Dr. Madison ran the practice alone.

Wagging his tail, Laddie wandered over to the senior Dr. Madison.

"You're a fine fellow, aren't you?" he asked, patting Laddie.

Laddie looked at him as though he were in complete agreement.

Dr. Madison set the chart he was carrying down on the counter and glanced at it. "Time for a rabies shot, I see," he said. "This won't take long." He took the syringe, prepared the shot, and administered it, all the while talking to Laddie in a soothing voice. Laddie didn't so much as flinch.

"He didn't act like he felt a thing. That's great," I told Dr. Madison.

"Coming up on thirty-five years now I've had to practice my technique." He laughed. "I see from the chart that you transferred records from a clinic in Kansas City. How do you like Lonesome Valley?"

"I love it! Of course, I'm upset about the poisonings, like everybody else. From what I understand, hemlock grows around here."

"It does, indeed. Nasty stuff. I treated one of the Equine Center's horses for hemlock poisoning a few months ago. There's no antidote, but luckily the horse survived."

"That's good. I wish Eric—you know, the man who died— had been so lucky."

"Did you know him?"

"Only slightly; he was a friend of my friend Susan Carpenter."

"Isn't she the artist who makes those life-size paper mâché animals?"

"Yes. They're great, aren't they?"

"Very striking. I thought about buying one for our waiting room, but I decided it would take up too much space. You don't happen to be an artist yourself, do you?"

"Yes, as a matter of fact, I'm a painter. I met Susan when I joined the Roadrunner."

"What kind of painting do you do? I mean, what are your usual subjects?"

"Expressionistic landscapes, mostly, and some pet portraits, too."

"I'd like to see them. I'll tell my wife we should stop in at the Roadrunner sometime and take a look."

"I have a website, too." I dug in my purse for my packet of business cards. The web address is right here," I said, handing him a card.

He thanked me, glanced at my card, put it into his pocket, and opened the door for Laddie and me.

"Well, what do you think of that, Laddie?" I asked as we drove home after stopping at the reception desk to pay the bill. "Is the doc really interested in my paintings or just being polite?"

In the back seat, Laddie panted happily, pleased with his outing, but his warm breath on the back of my neck held no clue as to whether the vet might prove a potential customer.

Chapter 20

After lunch, I intended to tidy the studio in anticipation of the evening tour. I hoped the mayor would show up, but since her assistant had told me how busy she was and I'd witnessed it myself when she'd been called away from the Roadrunner just as I was pitching her my landscape, I knew I couldn't count on it.

After I tidied the studio and cleared the floor, I removed my painting of Mr. Big from its hiding place in the closet and set it on an easel in the middle of the studio so that I could reach the hand-dyed scarves I'd stored in the back of the closet. I arranged a brilliant red tie-dyed scarf on a display bust and began hanging the rest of the scarves on a counter display that Dennis had made for me. It was the same type of clever wooden display stand that Belle had designed for me as an incentive for retailers who might want to sell my unique scarves in their shops.

I wasn't so absorbed in my task that I didn't notice Laddie jump up and run to the kitchen door. From the speed his tail switched back and forth, I knew Belle was my visitor. I rushed to put Mr. Big's portrait back into the closet and shut the door before joining Laddie to greet Belle.

"Laddie looks none the worse for wear," she said. When I looked confused, she added, "From his trip to the vet."

"Oh, right. He acted as though he didn't even feel a pinch when the vet gave him a shot. How's Mr. Big today?"

"He's fine. I think you were right about the gloomy weather. We were all feeling a bit tired and not very lively, but we're back to normal today. I brought you something."

She handed me a small bag. I peeked inside and found two plastic containers of fancy toothpicks, one green and one red for the holidays.

"Thank you! I forgot I'd run out of those. I don't know what I would have used for the cheese cubes tonight if you hadn't remembered."

"I almost didn't, but I was shopping at the party store, and I happened to see them on the shelf, and then I remembered that you were out of them."

"If I don't have any more people show up for the tour than I've had the last couple of weeks, we'll have to nibble the cheese and crackers ourselves. You are planning to come over tonight, aren't you?"

"I wouldn't miss it. I'd like to meet the mayor in person. I've only ever seen her on TV and at parades."

"I sure hope she comes, but there's no guarantee."

"If not, don't give up. You can always contact her again if she doesn't show."

"I know, but I don't want to make her feel that I'm harassing her like an obnoxious salesperson who won't take 'no' for an answer."

Belle grinned. "Amanda, there is no way anybody would tag you as an obnoxious salesperson. It's all right to show some persistence. She hasn't said 'no' yet, so don't give up until she does."

"OK, coach. You've convinced me."

"Good. Would you like me to bring any snacks for tonight?"

"No, I think I'm all set. I have the wine, cheese, and crackers, and I'll put out a tray of Christmas cookies, too."

"Don't forget to move the wreath from the front door to the studio door," Belle advised me.

"I'll do that right now, before I forget."

Belle and Laddie trailed me to the front door and back through the studio as I moved the wreath. Even Mona Lisa took notice and crept up behind Laddie to see what all the fuss was about. When I started to open the door, Mona Lisa looked a bit too interested. I definitely didn't want her exploring the great outdoors where she might get into all sorts of trouble. Mona Lisa was strictly an indoor kitty. I closed the door quickly, picked up Mona Lisa, and handed her to Belle, who cradled her in her arms while I hung the wreath. It took only a few seconds to position it perfectly, which was a good thing, because Mona Lisa was already struggling to get down.

"All set," I said, and Belle released Mona Lisa, who scampered off, into the living room. When we went back in, we found her perched on top of her kitty tree.

"I'd better get going," Belle said. "I just wanted to drop off the toothpicks, but I almost forgot to tell you that Dennis is going to string some Christmas lights on your hedge next to the sidewalk to the studio when he gets home from work. It'll add more of a festive air to the tour."

"That's great! I hadn't thought of that, but the hedge is a perfect place for lights, not that I have any myself. I didn't pack any Christmas decorations when I moved here. Ned has all our lights, wreaths, bulbs, and everything else at the house, probably just sitting there unused. I suppose Candy will want to use her own holiday decorations."

I started to choke up, remembering all the family Christmases we'd celebrated in that house, the home that Ned now lived in with Candy and their baby.

Belle gave me a gentle hug. "It's OK. You're doing fine here."

"I know," I said with a sniff. "Once in a while, my past life returns to haunt me, but, honestly, most of the time, I don't even think about it."

What I'd told Belle was true. I didn't dwell on the past, not like some of the divorced people I knew who constantly chattered about their ex-spouses, but every once in a while, a memory would hit me, along with a wave of nostalgia.

I shook off the melancholy moment and assured Belle that I was all right.

"You'll have a great holiday with Emma, Dustin, and your parents. It'll be your first Christmas in Lonesome Valley."

"That's true, and I'm looking forward to it."

"I know you'll all have a wonderful time."

"Thanks, Belle. You're a great morale booster. I don't know what I'd do without friends like you and Dennis. Tell him I'll have a chocolate meringue pie ready for him to take home after he strings the lights."

"You have his number. That's one of his favorites, although I have to say that he likes almost any kind of pie."

"He's not alone. We all have a sweet tooth."

"I admit I do. Life would be pretty routine without a little sugar once in a while, but you don't have to make pie this afternoon; tomorrow's soon enough. Don't you have to get ready for the studio tour?"

"No problem. I'll have the studio organized in a few minutes."

"All right, then. See you later."

As soon as Belle left, I finished tidying the studio. I decided to wait until after I finished my baking to rearrange the artwork that was displayed on the studio walls. Then I went to the kitchen to make two pies. I planned to send one of them home with Dennis and keep the other one so that Belle and I could each enjoy a slice sometime during the evening. As slow as things had been on tour night the past few weeks, we'd probably have plenty of time to indulge.

When I removed the pies from the oven, the sight of their just-right golden-brown meringues pleased me. I put them on racks to cool, on the kitchen counter before picking up Mona Lisa from the sofa, where she was snoozing. Laddie followed while I carried her into the studio and closed the door before setting her down on the floor. She protested with a loud meow, The studio wasn't Mona Lisa's favorite room, although she deigned to visit it occasionally. I would have left her in her comfy corner of the sofa if I'd stayed in the living room, but since I didn't trust her to stay off the counter when I wasn't around, she'd have to join Laddie and me in the studio so that I could keep an eye on her to make sure she stayed away from the Christmas tree and its enticing bulbs.

Mona Lisa quickly sized up the situation and decided that the only soft spot in the room was Laddie's bed. She plunked herself down in the middle of it and curled up while Laddie looked on. I knew he wouldn't disturb her. Instead, he lay down on the tile floor beside his bed, keeping a wary eye on the feline interloper.

The pies had cooled by the time I finished rearranging my artwork in the studio, and as I set them in the refrigerator, Mona Lisa leaped to the top of her kitty tree, looked down at Laddie and me with a smirk, and promptly turned her back on us. She ignored Laddie, not even bothering to turn around when he raced back through the studio door.

I peeked out and saw Dennis stringing lights on my hedge. Clipping Laddie's leash to his collar, I stepped out, with Laddie edging in front of me to greet his buddy, Dennis.

"Sorry, Laddie. No time to play right now," he said, as he petted my amiable retriever before returning to the lights. "I thought this string would work. It has the older, bigger multi-colored bulbs—no blinking lights. What do you think?" he asked me.

"It's a great idea."

"I can add another blinking, twinkling string if you like," he said, grinning at his own rhyme.

"No need," I said, as Dennis draped the lights over the hedge. "Those look perfect."

I shivered in the chilly air. I hadn't put a coat on before coming outside, but Laddie didn't mind the cold. He had his very own fur coat to keep him warm.

Chapter 21

A few minutes before six, I wheeled my tour sign out to the curb, turned on all the lights in the studio, and installed my baby gate in the door that led from my living room to the studio. Although Laddie could look into the studio, the gate discouraged him from coming in during Friday evening tour hours. He easily could have jumped over the gate if he'd wanted to, but he never tried.

When there were no visitors, I hung out in the living room, where I could see people arriving. Belle usually joined me, but she never brought Mr. Big on tour evenings because he raised a ruckus whenever people he didn't know showed up.

Belle came over soon after I'd set up.

"We had dinner, and I left Dennis alone with Mr. Big and your chocolate meringue pie. I'll bet half of it's gone by the time I go home."

"I made two pies, so we can have some later."

"Oh, good. I don't know how you always manage to get your meringue to come out just right. I've never been able to do it myself. Mine always browns unevenly or gets way too dark," Belle said, as she glanced out the living room window. "A car's parking in front. I think you may have a customer."

She paused, continuing to peek out the window. "She's coming up the walk now."

I stepped over the baby gate, into the studio, and Laddie jumped up to sit at the gate where he could observe the proceedings.

When the door opened, I had to hide my disappointment, because the woman who'd just arrived wasn't the mayor, but Cassie her assistant. Now that I saw her, I remembered she'd mentioned stopping by.

"Hello, again," she said. "Oh, what a darling dog!" She went straight to the gate to pet Laddie, who basked in her attention. "What's his name?"

"Laddie. I have a cat, too, but she makes herself scarce whenever visitors come."

"I wish I could have a pet. Unfortunately, my landlord has a strict no-pets policy. I may move when the lease is up, but it's hard to find an affordable studio apartment in Lonesome Valley. You have such a cute place here, and I love your studio. When I saw the card you sent the mayor, I knew I had to come and see it for myself." She looked around the studio. "Oh, there it is!" She left Laddie and went to have a closer look at the original painting. Cassie paused to take a breath before she asked how long I'd been painting. I'd barely had a chance to answer before she launched into a description of an art class she'd once taken.

I had the impression that not only did Cassie like to talk, but also that she was a bit lonely. Although she was an attractive woman of about thirty, evidently she lived alone. I was silently scolding myself for making assumptions when she confirmed what I'd thought.

"I came straight from work. I think I'll pick up a pizza on the way home. I wish I had some friends to go out with, but it's hard to meet people here in Lonesome Valley. I'll probably just watch TV all weekend," she said glumly.

"Have you lived here long?" I asked.

"No, only a couple of months. I got my job through my business college's placement service."

"I'm sure you'll meet some new friends soon. It just takes a while."

"I know," she sighed. "And everybody at work's so old, and they always have plans with their families every weekend, anyway. Like the mayor—she has three kids, and her husband runs his horse place and has that helicopter tour business. They're busy all the time."

"Did you say Bob Gibbs owns a helicopter business?"

She clapped her hand over her mouth. "Oops, I'm not sure I'm supposed to tell anyone that, because he's a silent partner." She air-quoted "silent." "But everybody knows about his other business. You've probably heard about it—the Equine Center?"

"Yes, I know he owns stables, and I think he gives some riding lessons, too."

"Uh, huh. I took one when I first got here, but he *charged* me for it. When the mayor suggested I take a lesson, I thought she was offering me a freebie. Anyway, my mistake, but it was my first and last since then. I can't afford riding lessons on my salary. You'd think she would have realized that."

Cassie definitely had a point. It sounded as though Melinda hadn't thought through her recommendation. As mayor, she'd certainly know how much the city was paying her assistant. Perhaps she had even set the salary herself.

Cassie seemed to be enjoying herself as she browsed through some of the prints I offered for sale and kept up a constant stream of chatter.

It was a bit of a relief when two couples came in. While I greeted them and answered their questions about my artwork, Cassie looked on as she nibbled one of the decorated Christmas cookies I'd set out. When it became obvious that the group wasn't in any hurry to leave, she headed for the door and departed with a quick wave.

One of the couples spent several minutes looking through my largest prints. They seemed interested, discussing where they might hang some of the artwork they were looking at, but, in the end, they decided against a purchase.

The other couple had separated, the man wandering from one painting to another, while he sipped wine. His wife skipped the wine and helped herself to cheese and crackers before she selected a tie-dyed turquoise scarf to purchase. So far, it was my only sale of the evening, but at least I'd sold something.

After the group left, I joined Belle, and we decided it was time for a dessert, so we each had a piece of chocolate meringue pie. I had tea with mine, and Belle opted for decaffeinated coffee. I slipped Laddie a snack, but since Mona Lisa didn't stir from her perch, I didn't dip into the kitty treats.

"The mayor's assistant is quite a talker. I could hear everything she said."

"She sure is," I agreed. "I think she's lonely."

"Sounds like it. Maybe Lonesome Valley is a bit too tame for someone her age."

"You know, that's pretty much what Mike Dyson told me once."

"The young cop who moved back to Phoenix?"

"Yes, that's the one."

"I guess our population may skew a bit older than some other places because lots of people retire here, but there's plenty to do."

We chatted for a while, and nobody else showed up. With only fifteen minutes remaining before tour hours officially ended at nine o'clock, I considered calling it quits for the evening, but, when I suggested closing to Belle, she urged me to wait until the bitter end. A few minutes later, I saw a pickup truck pull up in front of my sign and park.

"You were right," I told Belle. "Here we go again. Fingers crossed."

I went into the studio, taking care not to trip over the baby gate, and Laddie jumped up to see who was coming.

When the couple entered the studio, Laddie's tail whipped back and forth a mile a minute. He'd met one of the visitors once before, and he signaled his approval by getting up on his haunches and curling his paws under his chin.

Chapter 22

"How are you doing, fella?" Dr. Madison greeted Laddie with a pat on the head. He ran his hand over Laddie's shoulder and said, "No swelling; that's good."

"He's a handsome boy," the vet's wife said. "Your only dog?"

"Yes, he's my only dog, but I have a cat, too."

"Oh, lovely. I'm sorry. Where are my manners? I'm Katie Madison."

"Hi, Katie. I'm Amanda. Dr. Madison gave Laddie his rabies shot this morning."

"Jerry," he said. "Call me Jerry."

"OK, Jerry," I said, then turned toward his wife. "I bet you have some pets."

"We have three dogs—Minnie, Mickey, and Mighty. They keep us on our toes. Jerry showed me your card while we were at dinner tonight, and I told him I'd like to stop by. I'm afraid it's pretty near your closing time. I hope we're not too late."

"Of course not."

"Your card mentioned pet portraits. I thought we'd look at some of them."

"Over here." I led Katie to the wall where my portraits of

Laddie and Mona Lisa hung. Jerry stayed with Laddie, petting his furry patient.

"They're beautiful!"

"Most of the pet portraits I've painted have gone to their new homes." I lowered my voice and whispered, "I have another one of my friend Belle's dog hidden in the closet. Belle's in the other room right now, so I don't want her to find out. It's a Christmas present."

I motioned Katie to follow me, eased open the closet door, and flipped on the light so that she could see Mr. Big's portrait. Belle couldn't see into the studio from where she was sitting on the living room sofa, and I'd taken care to be especially quiet so that she wouldn't find out about the portrait prior to our gift exchange. I really wanted it to be a surprise. Luckily, Katie understood and nodded but didn't say a word until I'd closed the closet door.

"You don't happen to have any pictures with more than one dog, do you?" she asked.

"Not originals, but I have a print of a pair of bloodhounds." I rifled through one of the boxes of prints, all carefully matted and packaged in cellophane to protect them, until I found the print of the two dogs.

"Here it is." I held it up for Katie to get a better look.

"Jerry," Katie called, "come see this print."

Laddie looked disappointed at being thrown over for a picture as Jerry joined Katie and me.

"Very nice," he said.

"I think we should have a portrait of our little trio," she announced.

"Fine, but now might not be the best time to do it. The estimate for our new addition is running way higher than I anticipated, and I'm sure a custom portrait of three dogs doesn't come cheap." He spread his arms horizontally, then vertically, to show me the size of the canvas they'd need. "How much would something this size cost?"

When I quoted my price, Jerry raised his eyebrows and suggested "maybe next year" to Katie.

"I have a better idea," Katie declared. "Let's trade. The portrait for vet services in the same amount."

Jerry nodded. "We could do that. What do you think, Amanda?"

"I've never traded services before," I said, hesitating, since no cash would be forthcoming if I agreed to their proposed deal. Of course, no cash would be forthcoming if they didn't commission a pet portrait, either. On the other hand, I'd need vet services on an ongoing basis, and it would be nice not to have to pay a bill every time I took Laddie or Mona Lisa to the vet. "What about vaccines and medication? Would I have to pay the regular price for them?"

"No, just the wholesale. You'd pay exactly what we do for any meds," Jerry told me.

"Well, all right; it's a deal." I shook hands with Katie first, then Jerry. "I guess we should have something in writing."

"Sure," Jerry agreed. "If you wouldn't mind writing it up, I'll sign it. Just drop by the clinic anytime."

"OK, will do." I figured I could find some boilerplate language about trading online and adapt it to our situation. Although I wasn't the world's best when it came to business, I knew that a deal such as the one I'd just made ought to be in writing. Hopefully, we wouldn't encounter any glitches along the way, especially if the terms of our agreement were spelled out clearly.

Katie and Jerry didn't linger after we'd made our deal. I walked outside with them when they left to retrieve my tour sign and switch off the Christmas lights.

I still wasn't entirely sure the trade had been a good idea, but at least I wouldn't have to worry about paying any vet bills for a long time.

"Amanda, I'm proud of you," Belle said as I took down the baby gate and came into the living room. "It was smart to suggest a written contract."

"I'm learning, thanks to you, Belle. You really have a head for business. How about celebrating with a glass of wine?"

"Sure. I'll have a glass, but just one. The holiday calories are starting to pile up."

I retrieved the wine bottle from the studio and took a couple of my good crystal wineglasses from the cupboard, but, when I tipped the bottle to pour us each a glass, I found it was empty.

"Oops. I guess I spoke too soon. This bottle's empty. Only one guy even drank any wine tonight, and I thought he had just one glass. I didn't realize he polished off the entire bottle. I can open another one, though."

"That's all right. Let's skip it."

"Well, OK, if you're sure."

"I'm sure. I think I'll spend the calories on one of your Christmas cookies instead."

We each munched on a cookie as Laddie looked on enviously. I took pity on him and put a couple of baby carrots in his bowl, which suited him just fine. The minute I did that, Mona Lisa materialized, winding her way around my ankles and meowing loudly. I pacified her with a kitty-size tuna treat. When she'd eaten it, she stalked past Laddie and returned to her perch on her kitty tree.

"I'm kind of disappointed that the mayor didn't show up," Belle admitted.

"You and me both. It's going to be nice to have free vet services, but that doesn't pay the bills, and neither does one scarf sale. At least, a few people showed up this evening. It was definitely better than the last two weeks."

"Focusing the mayor's attention on your landscape again may not be as easy as I first thought," Belle said, "but it still could pay off if you could only touch base with her sometime when she's not distracted."

Belle had a point, and I promised myself I'd persist in my effort to arrange for her and the painting she liked to be in the same room in hopes that she'd decide to buy it.

It was nearly eleven by the time Belle went home. I was about to turn in for the night when I remembered I hadn't checked my phone since before the studio tour began. In fact, I had turned it off altogether so that I wouldn't be interrupted during tour hours. I turned it back on and waited until it came alive. After I checked my email and found nothing of interest, I checked my text messages and again found nothing significant. Then I listened to any voicemail messages.

I smiled as I listened to the first message I heard from Emma: "Hi, Mom. I forgot your studio tour is tonight. I'll call you tomorrow. Love you."

I poked the phone to move on to the next message, but it was an unsolicited sales pitch, so I deleted it immediately.

Finally, I scrolled through the list of calls. Only one caller hadn't left a message—only one caller tagged by my caller ID from the mayor's office at Lonesome Valley City Hall.

The mayor *had* called me, and I hadn't answered the phone!

Chapter 23

My stomach churned as I realized that I'd missed a chance to make a sale that could have kept my finances in the black for a couple of months. I admitted that I'd gotten my hopes up when Melinda had expressed interest in my paintings at the Roadrunner.

As Belle had suggested, I'd simply have to contact the mayor again, There was no point in dwelling on lost opportunity, but I wasn't in the best of moods when I went to bed, nor when I woke up the following morning, knowing I had missed an opportunity and not looking forward to attending a funeral in the afternoon.

Reflecting on the sad occasion, I felt glum, but my pets weren't about to let me get away with a down mood for long. They were as peppy as ever, anticipating the day ahead and, of course, a yummy breakfast.

After I fed them, I braced myself with some strong tea as I dawdled a bit over a muffin, but, finally, Laddie's eager anticipation of a morning walk kick-started me into action, so I dressed and took him for a leisurely stroll around the neighborhood.

I hadn't attended a funeral in years, not since my great-aunt had died. People didn't always wear black to funerals anymore, but I decided a dark color would be most appropriate, so, when Laddie and I got home, I pulled my navy suit out of the back of my closet and selected matching navy tights and shoes to wear with it. I left the ensemble out so that everything would be within easy reach when I was ready to go.

A few hours later, after I'd showered and dressed, I looked in the mirror and saw how severe I looked in my suit. I added a silver brooch and one of my abstract silk scarves in blue and green hues, and I was satisfied that the additions had softened my appearance.

Normally, I would have taken Laddie to Belle's for the afternoon, but, since she would be attending a Library Auxiliary meeting, Laddie would have to stay home with only Mona Lisa for company. My calico kitty was hiding under the sofa when I left, but Laddie accompanied me to the kitchen door, looking quite down as I prepared to depart.

"Be a good boy, Laddie, and take a nap," I said on my way out the door. With nothing else to occupy him, I felt sure he'd be sleeping before long.

When I arrived at the funeral home for Eric's memorial service, I was a bit surprised to see how many cars were in the parking lot. Inside, an usher was directing people, and I realized that Eric's wasn't the only service being held. A small sign by the door confirmed that I was in the right room, which was almost full. Perhaps Eric had been better known than I'd assumed, or maybe the fact that his hemlock-induced death was so unusual had drawn a crowd.

I hoped Susan had arrived before me, but, on first glance, I didn't see her. I did spot the police chief, sitting in the back row with Dave Martinez and Lieutenant Belmont. I walked slowly up the left aisle, looking for Susan, and finally found her sitting close to the front. The chair next to her had a coat draped over it, and I stepped gingerly in front of a few people, inching my way across the row of chairs, until I made it to my seat. Susan picked up her coat and placed it over the back of her chair as I sat down beside her.

"I guess I should have started out earlier," I whispered. "I had no idea it would be so crowded."

"Neither did I, but Eric's lived in Lonesome Valley his entire life, and he knew a lot of people, even though I don't think he had any really close friends."

We waited silently while soft music played in the background. From where we were sitting, I could see Josh and Kayla in the front row, along with Rebecca and Greg and a few other people I didn't recognize.

A pastor dressed in a black robe led the service. After prayers and a hymn, Josh took the podium to eulogize his uncle. Giving an elegant and well-crafted speech, he managed to hold himself together until he was almost finished, but he was choking on his own tears by the time he delivered the last line. He went back to his seat in the front row, where Kayla embraced him.

The pastor moved on quickly to invite others to share memories of Eric. For an awkward moment, nobody stood to come forward, but, then, just as I thought there wouldn't be another speaker, Josh's neighbor, Jack, stepped up and talked briefly about what a nice guy Eric had been. It struck me as a little odd since he'd told me he hadn't known him too well the night we'd discovered Eric's body.

Susan leaned over and said, "I think I should say something." When the neighbor had finished, she stepped forward and talked about Natalie and Eric, how much he'd missed his wife, and that they were together again.

Tears were streaming down her face by the time Susan finished speaking, and she struggled to compose herself after she came back to her seat.

There was a short lull, and it looked as though the pastor was about to continue the service, when I heard urgent, hushed voices behind me. I turned around to see what was happening, and I wasn't alone. Everybody within earshot had directed their attention to the arguing couple.

"Don't do it, Kevin. This isn't the place."

"Gina, I'm going to tell everyone what a low-down—"

"No, you're not! Quiet down. You're causing a scene."

Kevin shrugged and rose from his chair. His wife grabbed his arm, but he shook her hand off and marched to the front.

"They say not to speak ill of the dead," he proclaimed, "but I ask 'why not?' From what you've heard today, you'd think Eric Thompson was the greatest guy in the world. Well, I'm here to tell you that's a lie. He was a thief and a con man."

"Sir," the pastor said, flipping a switch to kill the mic, "that's most inappropriate. We're here today to celebrate a man's life." He attempted to take Kevin by the arm, but Kevin eluded his grasp. By this time, the chief and Sergeant Martinez were on their way to the front.

Kevin saw them coming and shouted, "I have a right to speak!"

"You've said enough," the chief told him. "I'm going to have to ask you to leave."

"Oh, yeah? Make me."

Since neither Sergeant Martinez nor the chief was dressed in his uniform, Kevin had no way of knowing they were police officers, but when Dave Martinez flashed his badge, Kevin backed down.

"Fine," he said. "I'll leave, but it doesn't change anything. Eric Thompson was a con man!"

As everyone looked on in shock, he stomped off down the aisle, but his wife didn't follow him, and the pastor calmly resumed the service, as though nothing untoward had occurred. After a final hymn and prayer to conclude the memorial, an usher led Josh, Kayla, Rebecca, Greg, and the others who'd been sitting in the front row out. He returned to dismiss the crowd, row by row, starting from the back, but it was slow going. Since Susan and I were close to the front, it was quite a while before we were invited to leave.

Right outside the door, Josh and everyone else who'd been sitting with him in the front row had formed a reception line to accept condolences.

After I'd expressed my sympathies to Josh, Kayla, and Greg, I came to Rebecca.

"Be sure to stop by our house for the reception," she said in a low voice. "I was going to ask the pastor to announce it, but, when I saw how many people were here, I knew there were too many for us to accommodate. I had no idea so many would show up."

Not wishing to delay the people behind me, I told Rebecca I'd be there and moved along, murmuring condolences to the others in the line, then stood aside and waited for Susan to join me.

"Are you going to the reception?" I asked her.

"I suppose so. Chip texted me about it before you came. I assumed they'd let everybody know, but it wasn't announced at the service. I wonder why."

"Rebecca told me they didn't expect such a big crowd, so she couldn't invite everybody because there wouldn't be enough room in the house."

"Yes, it was quite a tribute to Eric. Too bad his former partner had to show up."

Susan and I walked out to the parking lot together. I blinked in the bright Arizona sunshine, which felt all the brighter since we'd been inside, in a room with dim lighting.

"Uh, oh. There's Kevin over there. He didn't get too far after he left."

Kevin and Gina were engaged in a heated conversation. Finally, she'd had enough. Flouncing away from her husband, she climbed into the passenger seat of a large silver SUV and slammed the door. Kevin ignored her and turned his attention to the door through which Susan and I had just exited. He didn't have long to wait until Josh and his relatives came out.

Kevin rushed forward and confronted Josh. "You're Eric's executor, aren't you? He owed me money. You have an obligation to pay his debts."

"With what?" Josh asked. "He died bankrupt. This isn't the time or place to discuss it, anyway. Now, get out of our way."

Kevin planted himself firmly in Josh's path and crossed his arms.

"I'm not going anywhere!"

Chapter 24

"Suit yourself," Josh sneered, grabbing Kayla's hand and attempting to walk around Kevin, who moved to the side, blocking their path. I was afraid there was about to be a repeat performance of the altercation Kevin and Eric had had in the restaurant parking lot, but, once again, the police stepped in. The chief, Lieutenant Belmont, and Sergeant Martinez surrounded Kevin.

"Go home, or go to jail," the chief said firmly. "Your choice."

"All right; I'm leaving," Kevin growled. He pointed his finger at Josh. "You haven't seen the last of me. I want my money!" he yelled, as he backed away, then turned, and started off.

"I don't know what he expects me to do," Josh complained to Greg. "The estate's bankrupt, but I guess he doesn't believe me."

"Forget it, Josh. There's no way to satisfy him. You're doing the best you can."

"If the auction of Eric's household goods doesn't go well, there won't even be enough money to pay you back for final expenses," Josh said ruefully.

Greg shrugged. "Like I said, don't worry about it. Now, let's get going. We'll see you at the house."

Everybody drifted off to their vehicles then, and we formed a procession as we drove to Rebecca and Greg's house for the reception.

When I arrived at their house, Rebecca was setting out trays of food on her dining room table.

"Need any help?" I asked.

"I sure do," she told me. "Could you bring out everything that's sitting on the kitchen counter?"

"Right away." It didn't take us long to put out all the food. Meanwhile, Greg set up drinks in the kitchen, where he served them while Rebecca and I circulated in the living and dining rooms, taking drink orders. I estimated that there were probably about thirty people present. Although Rebecca and Greg's home was larger than mine, that many people were enough to make it crowded. No wonder Rebecca had decided not to announce the reception at the service.

After everybody had a drink in hand, I returned to the kitchen for an iced tea for myself. Rebecca was brewing another pot of coffee.

"I didn't make any food for this reception," she confided. "After the poisonings, I decided the safest bet was to buy it all at the supermarket deli. I don't want anybody thinking I poisoned them, if they go home with a tummy ache."

She jumped when a deep voice behind us said, "I wouldn't worry about it, Mrs. Winters. We're satisfied that none of your Pioneers group is responsible for the poisonings."

She turned and saw that the assurance had come from the police chief.

"So, we're in the clear?"

"Absolutely. We've talked to everybody in the Pioneers who contributed food for your booth, and it's clear that the poisoned carrot bars were left there by an outside party, not one of your members."

"That's a relief. I mean, I never thought that one of our own choir members could do such a thing, even by accident, but it did happen at our booth, and I feel bad about that."

"It sounds as though you don't think it was an accident," I commented.

"I'm afraid not. We're looking at some of the high school students who've been engaged in some dangerous pranks this semester, but I've probably said too much. Please keep that information to yourselves for a day or two while we finish our investigation."

We nodded as the chief helped himself to a mug of coffee and doctored it generously with sugar and milk before returning to the living room.

"Why do you suppose the police came?" Rebecca asked. "It sounds like they're on the way to solving the poisoning cases."

"They probably want to cover all the bases," I guessed. "You never know."

"So they want to see who shows up today?"

"I wouldn't be surprised."

"Well, I didn't see any high schoolers at the funeral home, did you?"

"No, I didn't."

"I hope they solve the case soon. To think that Eric may have died because of some stupid prank—"

We were interrupted then by several people who came into the kitchen for drinks. They helped themselves while Rebecca set out some more chilled bottles of beer, and I returned to the living room.

Josh, Kayla, and the relatives who'd sat with them in the

front row at the memorial service had huddled in one corner, rather than mingling with the guests. Nearby, Greg was explaining his relationship to the deceased to a group of people.

"He was my second cousin, once removed," he told them.

"I call myself cousin whether they're first, second, third, or removed," one woman noted. "It's easier that way."

"You've got that right," Greg agreed. "I guess that fits all Eric's relatives, except Josh."

I looked around and saw Susan and Chip with their heads together and Eric's neighbors, Jack and his wife, heading toward the dining room. Seeing Jack reminded me of the conversation we'd had the day I visited Sylvia Costa. I had a nagging feeling I was forgetting something as I mentally reviewed what Sylvia had told me.

Then I remembered. I'd thought, at the time, I should tell the police she hadn't gotten along with Eric. Since she was his next-door neighbor, there was a good chance the police had already interviewed her, but I could have kicked myself for not remembering sooner.

I looked around for Dave Martinez, since I thought he'd be the easiest one to approach about the matter, but I didn't see him. I went back into the kitchen, but he wasn't there, either. A few of the guests had departed, so I assumed Dave had left, too, but Lieutenant Belmont was sitting in a chair in the living room, observing the proceedings. Since I hadn't spotted the chief, either, I'd have to talk to the lieutenant.

He was juggling a plate piled with food, none of which qualified as part of the heart-healthy diet he was supposed to be following. The lieutenant was a stubborn man, and if he hadn't changed his diet after suffering a major heart attack and undergoing bypass surgery, I figured there wasn't anything I could say to convince him otherwise.

He must have read my mind, though, because, as I approached him, he put up his right arm as if he were directing me at a traffic stop.

"Don't say a word. I know what you're thinking," he grumbled.

"Oh? What am I thinking?"

"That I shouldn't be eating this stuff."

"Hmm."

"No comment? That's a first."

"Would you change your mind if I did comment?"

He snorted. "Not hardly."

"Well, then . . . . I actually wanted to talk to you about something else." I grabbed a folding chair and moved it closer to the lieutenant.

"I suppose you think you're onto the killer."

"No," I said, ignoring his sarcastic tone, "but I was talking to one of Eric's neighbors the other day, and she said something that I thought you should know about."

"All Mr. Thompson's neighbors have been interviewed, Mrs. Trent."

I shared my information, anyway.

"Sylvia Costa told you that she and Eric didn't get along? Lots of people don't get along with their neighbors, Mrs. Trent, but that doesn't mean they poison them."

He popped a pig-in-a-blanket into his mouth and practically swallowed it whole. Appalled, I watched as he stuffed in a couple more. If the lieutenant wasn't careful, he could very easily choke, but he appeared unconcerned as he chomped down two brownies in quick succession. Before I knew it, he'd eaten everything on his plate and had returned to the dining room for seconds or maybe it was thirds, for all I knew.

I stood and returned the folding chair to its previous position. Even though the lieutenant had made light of my information, I knew he'd look into it, but, of course, he never wanted to let on that he might take me seriously.

I really doubted that Sylvia had had anything to do with the poisonings. Despite the fact that she had knowledge of hemlock and even knew where to find it, and she was an accomplished baker, I simply couldn't picture her cooking up such a dicey scheme that involved slipping poisoned carrot bars into the Pioneers' booth, knowing that chances were slim that Eric would ever eat them and, at the same time, knowing that other people she had no grudge against would buy them. Anyone who would do that was surely a very sick or very evil person, and Sylvia didn't strike me as either.

I noticed that a few more people had said their goodbyes, and I thought it was time for me to be on my way, too. Laddie and Mona Lisa would be eagerly awaiting my arrival home, or, at least, Laddie would. I never knew about my mercurial calico cat.

I made the rounds, bidding the people I knew goodbye and offering condolences again to Josh. Susan and Chip were standing next to the front door, so I stopped for a word with them on my way out.

Chip, who normally would have made a point of flirting with me, acted very subdued.

"This is the first funeral I've ever attended," he confided. "Major bummer."

I wouldn't have put it that way myself, but sometimes I forgot how young Chip was, no older than my son Dustin. Certainly, Chip was a grownup, but he was so youthful that perhaps it wasn't too surprising that he had never attended a funeral before today.

Susan pulled me aside. "He's really down," she said.

"Yes, it's a sad occasion."

"I know, but he's talking about skipping the Roadrunner's Christmas party tomorrow evening."

"Party?"

I couldn't believe it, but I'd completely forgotten about the gallery's party. I'd been looking forward to spending Sunday at home, hanging out with my pets. Somehow, I just wasn't in the mood for a Christmas party.

Chapter 25

It was beginning to dawn on me that I'd been more than a little forgetful lately. I hadn't remembered to tell the police about Sylvia Costa's feud with Eric until seeing her neighbor, Jack, had jogged my memory, and the Roadrunner's Christmas party hadn't been on my radar, either, until Susan mentioned it.

Although I was aware that my financial woes had been weighing on my mind, I hadn't realized how much. I'd have to make a concerted effort to press on with my art career, despite the fact that December was shaping up to be a disappointing month sales-wise.

I reminded myself that my family would soon be with me to celebrate Christmas and that Brian would be home before New Year's Eve. I didn't want my concern over money to put a damper on our holidays.

Much as I hated to put everyday expenses, such as groceries or utilities, on my credit card, I'd very likely have to do that sooner, rather than later, despite my balance's creeping closer to my credit limit. Even though I'd known making my living as an artist would come with normal ups and downs in sales, adjusting to living with the reality of a roller-coaster income was more difficult than I'd ever imagined.

Unlike Lieutenant Belmont, who wouldn't be going home from the reception hungry, I'd been busy helping Rebecca, and I hadn't eaten anything there. My rumbling stomach reminded me that I'd skipped lunch, too, not something I often did, so, by the time I arrived home, I was ready for dinner, and my pets were more than happy to eat a little earlier than usual. I treated myself to a slice of the chocolate meringue pie for dessert and didn't worry about being too full now that I'd traded my navy suit and tights for pajamas and a robe. My fluffy slippers felt much more comfortable than the high-heeled shoes I'd worn to the memorial service. It was hard to believe I'd spent years wearing high heels to work every day when I'd assisted Ned at his insurance office. Now, casual attire was my norm, and my footwear usually consisted of sandals, sneakers, or moccasins.

Remembering that Emma had said she'd call me back today, I checked my phone, and, sure enough, she'd tried to connect with me during the memorial service. I called her immediately with apologies for not calling sooner. We chatted for more than an hour before she returned to studying. She had five final exams, all jammed into the first part of next week, and she claimed she wasn't planning on coming up for air until she'd finished them. I wished her luck, knowing that she'd do well. Emma had always been a good student, and she didn't choke at the prospect of taking a test. I couldn't wait to see her again. It would be only a few days before I'd be at Sky Harbor in Phoenix to pick her up. I called Dustin, but my call went to voicemail, and I realized that he was probably out on a date since it was Saturday night, so I decided to call him the next day. I always called my parents on Sunday, and I set the alarm on my phone to remind myself to call my son, too. Usually, that wouldn't have been necessary, but, as forgetful as I'd been in the last few days, I figured it couldn't hurt.

The next morning, after I'd walked Laddie and made my phone calls, I got to work in the kitchen, making the vegetable casserole and apple pie that I'd promised to bring to the Roadrunner's Christmas party, which was scheduled to begin at six, an hour after the gallery closed for the day. After I put the casserole and the pie into the oven to bake and set the timer, I had several free hours to spend in the studio, although Laddie coaxed me outside for a game of fetch and Mona Lisa kept bringing me her stuffed mouse, dropping it at my feet and waiting for praise. Once I picked it up, she always seemed satisfied. Sometimes, I'd hide it from her, behind the sofa or in some other out-of-the-way location. She invariably found it and never tired of the game.

I painted in my studio for a few hours, until it was time to get ready for the party. I dressed in a sparkly red sequined top and charcoal-gray, tailored wool slacks. Since the party was a pot luck in the meeting room of the Roadrunner, I thought that most members would dress casually, and, as it turned out, I was right.

Like me, many of the women wore a top that sparkled or shined, and some of them wore jeans, rather than dressier pants. There wasn't a skirt or a dress in sight. Others wore Christmas sweaters or even holiday sweatshirts. A few of the men wore sweatshirts and jeans, too, while others sported Christmas ties. Ralph, our oldest member, wore a spiffy red plaid vest.

Our utilitarian meeting room had been transformed for the party with swags of lights draped from hooks on the ceilings, holiday centerpieces on each table, and a huge Christmas tree in the corner.

A long table laden with food stood at the back of the room. I added my casserole and set my pie on the dessert table. Several of the small easels that the Roadrunner provided for students who took classes here were set up in the front of the room, and about half of them displayed a painting to be judged in the Roadrunner's holiday small works competition. Prizes consisted of certificates of achievement and vouchers for dinners for two at various restaurants around town, tiered by cost so that the first-place winner would be dining at one of the swanky restaurants at Lonesome Valley Resort, while the artists who won honorable mention received pizzas from Chip's father's pizza parlor.

Since I didn't normally produce paintings with dimensions of fourteen inches or less, I wasn't participating in the competition, but Susan had entered one of her small watercolors of yellow roses that looked like a winner to me.

I looked around for Susan and saw that she was placing a large bread basket on one of the tables in the back, I caught her eye, and she joined me. In the meantime, the rest of the easels were filling up, as members set up their artwork on them, but I didn't see any other paintings that I thought deserved first prize more than Susan's, and I told her so.

"Thanks, Amanda." I guess we'll have to wait until after dinner to find out if our judge agrees with you."

"Judge? For some reason, I thought the members were voting for the winners."

"Not this year, although we have done it that way in the past."

"Don't tell me Brooks Miller is going to judge."

"Brooks? No. I think Pamela asked one of the art teachers from the community college to judge the contest."

"Oh, good. I wouldn't have thought of Brooks except that I noticed him sitting over there with Pamela and Rich, and I wondered what he was doing here."

"Just a goodwill gesture, according to Pamela."

"I'm kind of surprised he came."

When I'd first moved to Lonesome Valley, Brooks had owned his own exclusive gallery off Main Street, featuring his own truly awful abstract art, and his wife had managed the place while he managed the Lonesome Valley Resort, which his family trust owned. He'd made it a practice to drop by the Roadrunner regularly to criticize our members' artwork. He'd been arrogant and obnoxious to say the least, but he'd since closed his downtown gallery and opened a new one in the Resort's shopping mall. Reinventing himself as an influential gallery owner, he'd booked several famous artists for shows at his new gallery, and he no longer displayed any of his own paintings. Along the way, he'd realized that he wasn't the great artist he'd thought he was, something his wife had cruelly pointed out to him when she'd announced she was leaving him.

The "new" Brooks was making an effort to get along with the rest of the art community in Lonesome Valley, and his gallery and the Roadrunner had participated in some joint events during the few months since he'd opened his current gallery. Even so, I couldn't imagine him as a judge of our contest, because his latest strategy depended on others' expert opinions. He offered gallery shows only to artists who were well established in their careers and widely acclaimed by critics.

"Where's Chip?" I asked. "I hope he didn't feel too depressed to come."

"He's coming with Josh and Kayla. He persuaded Josh that he needs a distraction, but I doubt they'll stay very long." She motioned toward the meeting room's rear door. "Here they come now."

Chip arrived, carrying a large covered pan, probably manicotti, a specialty of the pizza parlor, while Kayla carried a pretty, decorated cake that I was sure had come from the supermarket bakery, because I'd noticed one just like it there the last time I was grocery shopping.

Josh surveyed the room while he waited for Kayla and Chip to find a spot for the food they'd brought. Brooks looked up from his conversation with Pamela and Rich, saw Josh, and nodded. Josh waved to Valerie, one of our board members, who taught art at the high school, and I wondered whether she, like Sylvia Costa, had been one of his high school teachers.

Brooks had turned back to his conversation by the time Chip made room for the large pan of manicotti, but Rich had noticed Chip's arrival, and his face began to turn red as he started to stand up.

Chapter 26

Pamela tried to dissuade Rich by clutching his arm, but he leaned over and spoke to her, and she turned red, too. Brooks, caught in the middle of a situation he didn't understand, said something to Rich, and he finally sat down, but he didn't look happy.

Ever since Rich had insisted that Pamela resign as the director of the Roadrunner, Chip had gone out of his way to avoid being in the same room with her, so that Pamela could continue her job. Now, I feared their compromise might not survive the Roadrunner's party.

Chip ignored Rich and moved away from the food tables, which were close to where Pamela and Rich were sitting. Josh and Kayla, unaware of the tension, followed Chip to a quiet corner where they claimed a small table for themselves.

The incident hadn't escaped Susan's notice. "Maybe I shouldn't have encouraged Chip to come tonight," she said. "Do you think I should say something to Rich?"

"No, definitely not. Probably the less said, the better. Chip has every right to be here."

"I know, but I don't think he considered Rich when he decided to come. He's been so taken up with helping Josh since Eric died."

"Well, there's no reason for the situation to escalate. They can avoid each other for one evening easily enough."

Pamela had managed to compose herself by the time she invited us to help ourselves to dinner. She also introduced six members of the high school's choir, who'd been volunteered by their music teacher to sing following dinner.

Members appeared reluctant to start the line, so Pamela went first, breaking the ice, and several artists lined up behind her. I noticed that Rich and Brooks didn't make a move. I figured they were probably waiting until things settled down a little and fewer people were in line. Susan and I hung back, too. It would be easier to negotiate the buffet without worrying about jostling elbows.

Pamela helped herself to tiny portions of a few dishes before she took a quick glance at the dessert table and immediately dropped her plate.

Rich jumped up to help her. "Are you OK?"

She stared at the dessert table, while Dawn, who'd been standing behind her in line, scooped up the fallen plate and food and discarded them.

"Look at that," Pamela said. Her hand trembled as she pointed to something on the table, but, from our vantage point, Susan and I couldn't tell what it was.

Dawn could obviously see it, though, and she motioned for her husband to take a look.

He picked up a plate from the dessert table and tipped it enough so that we could all see the plate of carrot bars he held.

At this shocking revelation, everyone began talking at once, but Dave quieted the crowd with a simple request. "Folks, I'd like to talk to whoever brought this dessert."

Silence followed.

"I'm going to get to the bottom of this, one way or another. If you know who brought these carrot bars, speak up now."

"She did it!" a teenager said, pointing to the girl who was sitting across the table from him—a table occupied by six high schoolers wearing identical blazers.

The girl shot daggers at her classmate, but she kept quiet.

I thought she looked awfully familiar. I decided I must have seen her at the crafts fair the previous weekend.

"Is that true, miss?" the sergeant asked.

"What if it is? They're just carrot bars. It's not like they're poisoned or anything."

Admirably cool and collected as usual, Dave suggested the gallery members continue with dinner before he escorted the girl out into the hallway.

We did as Dave had suggested, although the incident had put a damper on the festivities. I couldn't help but notice that Josh had followed them out of the room, and Chip had accompanied his friend.

I could only imagine what was going on in the hallway. We heard raised voices a few times, but we couldn't make out what was said.

Finally, Josh came back in, a disgusted look on his face, and returned to his seat next to Kayla. Chip showed up a minute later, and Susan waylaid him before he had a chance to rejoin Josh and Kayla.

"What happened?" Susan asked.

"The kid claims her grandmother made the carrot bars because she asked her to. She says her grandmother just got back from vacation and didn't know anything about the poisonings. For some reason, the girl thought it would be funny to scare everybody, or, at least, that's what she told Dave. I have the feeling there's more to it, like maybe a dare from her friends. Who knows? Anyway, by the time Dave finished talking to her, she changed her tune and started blubbering. I guess she's not as smart as she thinks she is."

"What's going to happen to her now?" I asked.

"Dave's taking her home. He asked me to let Dawn know he'd be back later. Of course, he's going to have the carrot bars analyzed, too, but I could tell he doubts that they've been poisoned."

"What an incredibly stupid stunt!" Susan said. "Whatever was that girl thinking?"

Chapter 27

We might never know her true motive, but the damage had been done. The misguided high schooler's reminder of the poisoning zapped the vitality from the rest of the party. Despite Pamela's efforts to carry on, the event wrapped up earlier than usual, but not before I had a welcome surprise when Melinda Gibbs called me as the party was breaking up. It was so noisy in the meeting room that I hurriedly stepped into the hall so that I could hear the mayor.

"Amanda, I'm so glad I caught up with you at last. I intended to come to your studio tour Friday night, but something came up. I'd love to see your painting in person. Could you bring it to the house tomorrow morning early, before I go to the office? Say eight o'clock?"

Of course, I jumped at the chance to show Melinda my painting at last. She hung up before I thought to ask her directions to the ranch where she and her family lived, but I had a general idea of its location, and, since her husband's Equine Center was on the same property, I'd likely find a map on the Center's website.

I was so excited I could hardly sleep that night. Since I wasn't getting much sleep anyway, I rose early and took Laddie for a morning walk. I wanted to tell Belle the good news, but it was way too early to rouse my friend.

The landscape I was taking to Melinda's home was quite large, and I struggled to get it into the back of my SUV because it was so bulky.

With the help of my phone's GPS directions, I had no problem finding the place. A sign marked the lane to the Equine Center that forked off from the gravel road to the house. I pulled up in front of the home, a typical southwestern style with stucco walls and red tile roof.

Melinda met me at the front door. Although it wasn't easy to juggle the unwieldy canvas, Melinda made no attempt to assist me, as she ushered me through her huge living room to an equally large den, where I could smell the faint odor of fresh paint. The bare walls, painted a rich cream color, provided a perfect backdrop for dramatic artwork. Centered above the sofa, my expressionistic landscape would make an excellent focal point for the room. I hoped Melinda would come to the same conclusion.

"Let's see how it would look above the sofa," she said.

I hoisted the canvas, making sure that the wire on the back of it caught firmly on the large screw centered above the sofa, but I could feel it give the moment I relaxed my grip slightly. Thankfully, I hadn't let go of the painting, or it would have come crashing down.

"Oh, no. I'm afraid you're going to need a larger hook or screw that's anchored in a stud to hang anything here."

"All right. I can't tell how it would look there without seeing it in place. Can you just hold it steady so I can look at it from back here?"

I attempted to do as she asked, but holding the canvas

proved too much for me. "I'm sorry, but I need help. Maybe you could hold up the other end," I suggested.

"How am I supposed to see how it looks then? Oh, never mind. I'll go get Bob."

She stepped into the hallway, and I heard a faint knock on a door, followed by the murmur of voices and the sound of the door closing. Melinda returned to the den.

"He's on a business call. I'll have to get my son. He's feeding the horses. Wait here. I'll try to hurry him up."

She threw on a coat that had been draped over one of the chairs in the den. I watched from the large plate-glass window as she walked toward the equestrian center. I could see a man coming out of the stables, leading a horse. On second glance, I recognized him as Eric's neighbor, Jack. I wondered whether he boarded a horse at the Equine Center, but since I was beginning to regret having drunk an entire pot of tea, and, starting to feel desperate, I didn't take time to speculate further. I glanced into the hallway and saw an open door on the right. Luckily, it turned out to be a powder room, and I quickly availed myself of the facilities.

The door across the hall was closed, but I could hear a man's voice, and I surmised that the room was the office of the mayor's husband. I wished the door were open so that I could see Ralph's painting, the one Melinda had purchased at the gallery the same day she'd indicated her interest in one of my landscapes.

I would have returned to the den immediately, but I noticed that Bob's voice seemed louder than it had earlier. Perhaps he'd moved around the room while he was talking, but what caught my attention most was Bob's mention of Eric's name. I froze right outside the door.

"You should have taken care of this. We can't have that Thompson kid finding out about it. Do the same as you were going to do with Eric. Tell the nephew you took the case in good faith but that, on further investigation, you've concluded it's a loser."

Evidently, Bob had changed the setting of his phone to speaker so he could move about the room because I could hear the response loud and clear.

"I'm handling it," a terse voice said.

"See that you do. I'm paying you enough."

"Not nearly as much as I'd make from my contingency fee if I won the case."

"That won't do you any good if I'm bankrupt like Eric. Take what you can get and call it a day."

I didn't wait to hear any more. Despite the carpet on the floor, I tiptoed back to the den so that Bob wouldn't realize I'd heard part of his conversation.

I didn't have time to collect my thoughts because Melinda and her son, a gangling young teenager, showed up mere seconds after I did.

"Bobby, help Ms. Trent hold that painting up over the sofa so that I can see how I like it there."

Bobby, who was stronger than he looked, easily lifted his end of the painting. We held it in place for what seemed forever, while Melinda viewed it from different angles around the room. Finally, she motioned for us to lower the canvas.

"I think it will do nicely," she said. My excitement over the sale was tempered by what I'd heard her husband say, but I wasn't about to turn her down. Maybe I had misunderstood what Bob meant, but I had a feeling that wasn't the case. I waited while Melinda wrote me a check and then thanked her.

"Wait a minute. The painting will definitely need to be framed. I don't have time to deal with it today. Could you drop it off at the frame shop at the Resort and tell Brooks I'll be in tomorrow to select a frame?"

"Yes, I can do that." I could almost hear her say "there's a good girl" in a patronizing way, but, of course, my imagination was running away with me.

It wouldn't be fun lugging the weighty canvas through the Resort's mall to get to Brooks's frame shop, located next door to his gallery, but, at this point, I didn't want to do anything that might cause Melinda to change her mind.

I drove straight to Lonesome Valley Resort, dropped off the canvas, and got a receipt from one of Brooks's assistants. On the way home, I stopped at the bank and deposited Melinda's check. Normally, I would have felt ecstatic after making such a big sale, and the timing of it couldn't have been better, but the knowledge that Melinda's husband was trying to manipulate legal proceedings both shocked and angered me, and I knew I'd have to tell someone about it, but who?

The chief, the local bar association, Josh? Or maybe all three.

Chapter 28

Belle was coming out of her house with Mr. Big tugging on his leash, but the little dog wasn't making much progress since Belle was stronger than he was, but that didn't stop him from trying.

I waved as I pulled into my driveway. When I parked in my carport, Belle and Mr. Big came to greet me.

"How did it go with the mayor?" she asked.

"She bought my painting."

"Great news! Why don't you look happier?"

"Oh, Belle, I found out something that, well, let's just say it upset me, Come in, and I'll tell you all about it."

"Do you mind if we go for a walk? Mr. Big's been antsy since I got up this morning. Some exercise will do him good."

"Sure, let's do that. Laddie's always up for a walk." He'd had one earlier, but the more, the better, as far as he was concerned. "I'll just be a second."

I went into the kitchen while Belle waited outside for me to return with Laddie, who was, indeed, raring to go. He joyfully greeted his pal, and we started on our way.

Belle could barely contain herself as she waited for me to explain why I wasn't jumping up and down with glee over having sold one of my most expensive works.

I launched into my story and told Belle everything I'd heard Bob Gibbs say. "The man he was talking to has to be Eric's lawyer. He must be Josh's lawyer now. According to Chip, he's already indicated that the case isn't worth pursuing. The guy told Bob he was 'handling it.'"

"I'm confused," Belle said. "Why would the mayor's husband be involved in any of this?"

"Remember the mayor's assistant who came to my studio tour on Friday?"

"Sure, the lonely young woman."

"Right. You may not have heard everything she said, but she told me that Bob Gibbs was a silent partner in a helicopter tour business. Emphasis on 'silent,' I guess, because then she indicated that she probably shouldn't have told me that."

"I see. The helicopter tour company may have been responsible for Eric Thompson's wife's death. I wonder why Eric waited so long to bring the suit."

"According to Susan, he hadn't been functioning very well since his wife Natalie's death in the crash. Evidently, he hadn't decided until lately that he'd sue. We think he wanted to show Susan a copy of the lawsuit the night we found him. He'd told her he expected to come into a great deal of money soon."

"Sounds as though that lawyer encouraged him."

"Yes, it does, but, I'm guessing that when Gibbs found out from his partner that the company was being sued, he must have decided to bribe the attorney. Eric's death came at an opportune moment for him because Josh didn't know anything about the lawsuit. He only knows whatever Eric's lawyer has told him."

"What are you going to do?"

"I think I should report it to the police and Josh, too. What do you think?"

"I agree. Hopefully, the police can get to the bottom of it, and Josh can get himself a different lawyer."

An hour later, I was climbing the six steps to the door of the police station. A young uniformed officer I didn't recognize sat at the reception desk, but Dave Martinez was coming down the hallway as I entered, so I bypassed the young officer and waved to catch Dave's attention.

"Hi, Amanda. What's up?"

"I have a bit of a dilemma. I overheard . . . ." I stopped and looked around. The officer who was sitting at the reception desk didn't act as though he were paying any attention to us, and there was nobody else around except the three of us, but, just to be on the safe side, I motioned for Dave to come closer and lowered my voice to a whisper. I repeated what I'd heard of the conversation Bob Gibbs had had with Eric's—now Josh's—lawyer.

After listening attentively, Dave rubbed his chin and said, "Amanda, this situation is above my pay grade. Considering who's involved, I think you'd better talk to the chief. Come on back."

He led me down the hallway to the chief's vacant office and asked me to take a seat while he went to find the chief. I'd never been in the chief's office before, but it was obvious from the no-frills room that he didn't care about the trappings of his office. "Bare-bones" and "no-nonsense" probably best described his style. My mind wandered as I sat there, waiting for him. I was wondering what had happened with the high school girl who'd thought bringing carrot bars to the Roadrunner's Christmas party would somehow be funny when

Dave popped in to tell me the chief would be with me in about five minutes.

"Would you like some coffee while you wait, Amanda? I can grab you a cup."

"No, thanks, Dave. I'm fine. I was just thinking about that girl who blew up our party Sunday night. Is she a part of the group being investigated?"

He raised his eyebrows. "You know about that?"

"I was there when the chief mentioned it to Rebecca at the reception Saturday afternoon."

"I'm surprised he said anything about it."

"He probably wanted to reassure Rebecca that none of the Pioneers had any involvement. She feels terrible that they sold those carrot bars, even though they had no way of knowing they were poisoned."

"It's still under investigation; that's about all I can say. The chief may be willing to tell you more, but we haven't made any arrests yet. Believe me, you would have heard about it if we had. The reporters from our local media call constantly for updates."

A few minutes later, as if to confirm what Dave had just told me, the chief came in, his cell phone to his ear.

"You can expect a press release this afternoon," the chief said, ending his conversation. He took a seat behind his desk and set his cell phone down on top of it. "What's this Dave's been telling me about Bob Gibbs?"

I repeated my story, trying to remember the conversation I'd heard word for word. I couldn't quite do that, but I managed to convey the gist of it accurately.

"Are you absolutely sure that's what you heard?"

"I wouldn't be here if I weren't."

"I don't have to tell you that the Gibbses wield some power

in Lonesome Valley. The mayor's my boss, as a matter of fact, and Bob knows plenty of other influential people, so the situation is a political nightmare, to say the least."

After hearing those words, I wondered whether the chief would investigate.

"You understand that what you've given me would be considered hearsay in court. The district attorney would need some solid evidence before bringing charges."

"So you're not going to investigate?"

"I didn't say that. I'm going to have a talk with Bob, and we'll see what he has to say for himself. You have no idea who the lawyer was that Bob was talking to?"

"None. He never called him by name. He put the call on speaker, and I could tell that it was a man's voice, but Josh can give you that information."

"It sounds as though that young man needs to find himself a new lawyer."

Chapter 29

I couldn't have agreed more. If Josh could find a lawyer willing to take the case and the attorney succeeded in either winning the judgment in court or negotiating a settlement, Josh should be able to settle Eric's estate and perhaps have an inheritance for himself. All in all, such a potential outcome would be much more favorable for him than the status quo.

Still, I hesitated when I thought about calling him because I'd observed what a quick temper he'd displayed on the night of his uncle's demise. I decided to enlist Chip's help. After all, the two had been good friends for years, and, if Josh became upset at the news, Chip would probably have better luck calming him down than I would.

I phoned Chip, explained that I had important, but possibly upsetting, news for Josh, and asked him if he'd be willing to be there when I spoke to his friend. "It's just that I've seen that he has a temper. I was hoping you might be able to talk him down if he gets upset."

"So it's bad news?" Chip asked.

"I'm afraid it's the 'I-have-good news-and-I-have-bad-news' dilemma. I should probably leave it at that for now."

"OK, Amanda, you're in luck. I'm at the Pizza Place, and

Dad's gone home for a few hours. Business is really slow this time of the day. I asked Josh to join me for a late lunch. He should be here in a few minutes, so why don't you come over right now?"

"All right. I can do that."

"I have an extra-large supreme in the oven for Josh and me. What can I make for you?"

Chip's offer reminded me that I hadn't had lunch yet, so I gave him my order. "A mini-mushroom pizza would hit the spot."

"One mini coming right up."

"Thanks, Chip. I'll be there in a few minutes."

"See you, soon, Beautiful."

Happy that Chip was acting more like his usual self, I drove to the Pizza Place and noticed that there were only a couple of cars in the parking lot.

Taking my sunglasses off, I went inside and tried to adjust my eyes to the darkened interior.

"Ah, the woman of the hour." Grinning at me, Chip stood behind the counter, next to the cash register. He turned and called into the kitchen. "Hey, Don, answer the phone and cover the counter, please."

He led the way to a corner booth where we'd be well away from the entrance and the counter. "Let's sit here," he said. "I'll have to leave if someone wants a delivery. Don and I are the only ones holding down the fort until Dad comes back later. It probably won't happen this time of day, though."

"I understand. You have to take care of business."

"Josh should be here any minute. How about cluing me in?"

"Well, all right."

"Never mind. Here he comes now."

I looked out the window and saw the same red sports car that Josh had been driving when he and Kayla arrived at his uncle's house the night we'd found that Eric had been poisoned.

Chip greeted his friend at the door and told him I needed to talk to him. From the look on Josh's face, I knew he doubted I could tell him anything of interest. I couldn't really blame him. After all, it was pure coincidence that I'd heard Bob Gibbs talking to Josh's attorney.

Nevertheless, he greeted me politely and settled himself opposite me in the booth. Chip asked what we'd like to drink. Josh opted for a beer, while I asked for diet cola.

Chip was back with our pizzas and drinks before the silence between Josh and me became too uncomfortable. I noticed that Chip was having cola, too, rather than beer, like Josh, probably because his father depended on him to make deliveries. Chip sometimes seemed careless or nonchalant, but I knew his dad could rely on him, although perhaps that hadn't always been the case.

When Chip slipped into the booth on my side, I slid over and took a quick bite of pizza and a sip of my diet cola before I began to relate my story. "Josh, I wanted to talk to you today because I overheard something that concerns you."

"OK."

"It has to do with the lawsuit your uncle was planning on pursuing against the helicopter company that was involved in his wife's death."

"Poor Aunt Nat. It was such a terrible crash. From what I understand, nobody could possibly have survived it. I thought the consensus at the time was that the crash was weather-related and the pilot did nothing wrong. That's why I was kind of surprised Uncle Eric decided to sue."

"Actually, I don't know any of the details of the accident or the merits of the case, but this has to do with somebody trying to influence the filing."

"Go on."

"From what I overheard, Bob Gibbs plans to pay off your lawyer to drop the case."

Josh frowned. "Who's Bob Gibbs? I've never heard of him."

"He's the mayor's husband," Chip interjected. "He runs those stables north of town, and he has some other local business interests."

"I don't get it," Josh said. "Why would this Gibbs guy care about the lawsuit?"

"Because he's one of the owners of the helicopter tour business, a silent partner, according to the mayor's assistant. And, by the way, after she revealed that, she admitted that she shouldn't have told me, so I assume it's meant to be a secret."

Josh stared at me. "Wow! You really get around. It's amazing." Brian had once told me I was amazing, too, only there was a difference. Brian admired me, while Josh probably had me pegged as a middle-age meddler and not much else. "Phil Babcock already told me Eric didn't have much of a case, but he didn't say he was going to drop it altogether."

"I bet that's coming," Chip said. "He probably doesn't want to make it sound too sudden. Could be he's trying to soften you up."

"Chip may be right," I agreed. "The lawyer said 'I'm handling it.' Those were his exact words."

I could almost imagine steam rising as Josh took in the ramifications of the conversation I'd overheard.

"We'll see about that," he said angrily. "Just point me in this Gibbs guy's direction. I'll take care of my so-called lawyer later."

"Whoa! That's not going to help the situation," Chip warned.

"The police are investigating," I chimed in.

"The police?" Josh looked at me incredulously. "You really *do* get around!"

"Let them handle it, Josh," Chip suggested. "In the meantime, you can hire another lawyer."

Josh didn't respond right away. At least, he was thinking about his options. Finally, he nodded.

"You may be right. I need to find a lawyer Gibbs can't influence. Maybe someone in Phoenix."

"That sounds like a good idea. There are plenty of personal injury lawyers there. Hold on; it looks like Don needs something. I'll be right back."

Chip jumped up and went to the counter to speak to Don, a gray-haired man wearing a white apron and cap.

When Chip came back to the booth, he told us he had to make a delivery.

"I'd better be going, too," I said, as I slid out of the booth's faux leather bench seat.

"Thanks for telling me about this, Amanda," Josh said. "I appreciate it."

"You're welcome. I'm sorry to be the bearer of bad news, but I thought you should know what's going on."

Chip grabbed the pizza box Don had set on the front counter, and we walked out to the parking lot together. When I looked back, I could see Josh through the window with his cell phone to his ear. I guessed he wasn't wasting any time trying to locate a new lawyer, or perhaps he'd called Kayla to let her know what he'd learned about his lawyer.

As I drove home, I reflected that it had seemed like a very long day, mainly because the stress was getting to me.

Normally, after selling a painting, such as the one Melinda had purchased this morning, I would have felt thrilled, but, thanks to her husband's bribery scheme, I felt rather depressed and anxious. I was relying on my pets to lighten my mood when I got home, and they didn't disappoint me.

Laddie and Mona Lisa were both waiting for me at the kitchen door when I opened it. Mona Lisa dropped her toy mouse at my feet and meowed loudly until I picked her up while Laddie danced joyfully around me, stopping for a pat and then continuing to bounce around me.

After a few minutes in my arms, my calico kitty had had enough. She jumped down and scampered into the living room, but, instead of springing to the top of her kitty tree, she settled herself on the wide arm of my chair.

I stooped to give Laddie a hug, and he trailed me around my tiny house until I took him outside for a game of fetch. He ran and leaped, expertly catching his ball every time I threw it. I played with him for quite a while before dusk settled on us and we went inside. Mona Lisa hadn't moved from the arm of my chair. I thought she was sleeping when I sat down beside her, but she proved me wrong by quickly moving into my lap. She shot a look of disdain at Laddie, who was sitting next to the chair, resting his chin on the other arm. He whined softly until I began to stroke his head.

I realized the stress of the day was fading as I relaxed with my pets. I put the foot rest up, and, before I knew it, I'd fallen asleep. I didn't awaken until Laddie persistently nudged me with his nose. My golden boy was telling me it was time for dinner. I glanced at the clock on the side table next to the sofa and saw that he'd been a very patient dog, indeed. It was an hour past dinnertime.

Mona Lisa got into the act and began batting my other arm with her paw.

"OK, OK. Dinner is coming right up." My assurances satisfied my pets, who eagerly followed me into the kitchen. I dished up their food, set their bowls at opposite ends of the kitchen as usual, and reheated some leftovers for my own dinner.

My cell phone rang just as the microwave dinged. I looked at the caller ID on the display and gulped in dismay.

"Hello?" I said as brightly as I could manage, considering the fact that I knew I wasn't going to like what I heard.

Chapter 30

"Ms. Trent, my husband had a visitor this afternoon," the mayor said. "Care to guess who stopped by?"

Although I felt sure Melinda referred to the chief, I didn't answer. I didn't have much of a chance to speak, anyway. She barely paused before continuing.

"No? It was our very own chief of police, asking outrageous questions. It seems that somebody's been eavesdropping on private conversations. Now, I wonder who that could be."

I couldn't believe that the chief had outed me as his source. Then, again, maybe he hadn't. Considering that I'd overheard Bob Gibbs's conversation with Josh's lawyer in the morning and that the chief had talked to him only a few hours later in the afternoon, it was equally possible that Melinda and her husband had put two and two together to conclude that I'd informed the chief of the conversation.

"Still nothing to say, Ms. Trent? Well, I do! How *dare* you? You were a guest in my home. You had no right to go sneaking around."

"I wasn't sneaking," I protested.

"Whatever. Now you hear me, and you hear me good. Don't you *ever* come near me or my family again. I promise you you'll regret it if you do. And one more thing: I will never display your painting in my home. I don't want it. You can tear up my check."

"Unfortunately, I can't do that. I've already deposited it."

"In that case, I'll have my bank put a stop payment on it," she snapped. "You'll never get a penny."

The line went dead immediately. Melinda had hung up.

I stared at the cell phone in my hand for a few seconds before setting it down on the kitchen counter. Frankly, Melinda's call hadn't come as a total shock. It had occurred to me that, if she connected me to the chief's investigation of her husband, she wouldn't be too happy with me, to say the least. Even so, I'd harbored a hope that she wouldn't realize that the tip had come from me.

Due to the loss of my only significant sale of the month, I was right back to square one as far as my finances were concerned, and square one wasn't a very good place to be. Although my situation didn't qualify as end-of-the-world serious, I knew that, if sales didn't pick up soon, I'd probably have to ask my parents for a loan. How embarrassing! Even though I knew they'd be happy to help, I'd never borrowed money from them, and I really didn't want to start now, at age fifty, when I should be able to take care of myself.

Belle commiserated with me when I called to tell her that the mayor had canceled my sale.

"Do you think Melinda knows what her husband's up to, or is she defending him solely based on loyalty?" I asked Belle.

"Good question. I suppose a person could hide something like that from a spouse, but it wouldn't be easy. My best bet is that she knows. After all, if he's having money problems, it'll affect their entire family eventually. She'll most likely do her best to make sure nothing comes of the investigation."

"I'm beginning to doubt that the chief will get very far. There may not be any evidence to uncover, especially if both men deny Bob offered the lawyer a bribe and no payment's been made yet. I know they can't do anything on my word alone. The chief reminded me that the conversation I overheard would be classified as hearsay in court, but I have a feeling it will never go that far."

"Probably not, but, Amanda, be careful. You've made an enemy of the mayor."

"I know, and I hope she doesn't take it out on the Roadrunner. The Gibbses have always been big supporters of the arts here in Lonesome Valley."

"You told me Melinda bought one of Ralph's paintings. She hasn't returned that, too, has she?"

"I didn't think about that, but not as far as I know. At least she didn't mention it."

"Well, her beef is with you. She has nothing to gain by snubbing other artists, so I wouldn't worry about that too much. Anyway, she's already hurt you by canceling the sale of your painting. That's quite a blow in itself."

"I'll say."

I felt drained after what had been a very trying day, but my only play was to accept what had happened and move on. Moping about a lost sale certainly wouldn't solve my money problems.

When Brian called me later, I tried my best to sound cheerful, but I wasn't as successful as I'd hoped. It didn't take him long to discern that something was wrong.

"What is it, Amanda? Aren't you feeling well? You don't sound like your usual self."

That's all it took for me to blurt out the entire story while he listened patiently.

"You did the right thing in reporting what you heard to the police," he said. "I'm sorry it cost you."

"Me, too. I was counting on that sale to carry me through the next couple of months."

"I know it's tough when you don't have a regular paycheck coming in. I've certainly always relied on mine. I don't think I could do what you do, but I admire you for it. You're doing what you love and making a living from your artwork."

"Well, trying to make a living from it, anyway."

"Things will pick up," he said optimistically.

"I hope so."

"In the meantime, I'd be happy to make you a loan."

"Oh, no, Brian. I couldn't possibly accept a loan, but I appreciate the offer."

"It still stands, if you change your mind."

If I asked anyone for a loan, it would be my parents, although I was holding onto a ray of hope that it wouldn't become necessary. Accepting a loan from Brian wouldn't get our budding relationship off to a very good start, in my opinion. And what if it didn't pan out between us? Owing him money would only complicate things further. No, borrowing money from Brian definitely was a bad idea. No doubt about it.

Chapter 31

By the following day, I hadn't changed my mind about accepting a loan from Brian. I didn't want to owe any of my friends or relatives money. Of course, the same caveat didn't apply to the bank that issued my credit card. I calculated that, between my meager checking account and the amount I could charge on my credit card, I would make it through the holidays, when I'd be spending far more on groceries than usual since I'd have company.

Utility and insurance bills would come due after the first of January, and I decided it would be better to borrow from my parents than to fall behind on my bills.

With that decision made, I went on to the next item of business, which was preparing my contract with Jerry Madison. I did a little research online and came up with a simple contract that clearly spelled out the terms of our agreement. Although I didn't usually take Laddie with me when I ran errands, I decided to bring him along and stop to walk him at one of the large parks on the other side of town before we came home.

Seeing me grab my purse, Laddie gave me the same sad look that he always displayed whenever I left him home alone with Mona Lisa, but, as soon as I picked up his leash, his attitude changed immediately. He could barely contain his excitement when I snapped on his leash and led him outside to our waiting chariot.

Laddie recognized the vet's office right away when I pulled into the parking lot. I didn't have to coax him out of the back seat; he jumped down, happy to come with me. He'd never had a bad experience at the vet's, so he had no reason to hesitate. Of course, I'd never leave him alone in the car.

When I approached the receptionist, she smiled at Laddie and asked when his appointment was scheduled. I explained that I needed to drop off some paperwork for Dr. Madison to sign.

"I'll make sure he gets it, but he's really busy this morning. Would you like me to call you when it's ready?"

"That would be fine." I'd hoped to take care of it right away, but I could see that the office was busy. Several pet parents with their dogs or cats were sitting in the clinic's waiting room. "Here's my cell phone number." I circled it on my business card and handed it to her.

We couldn't get back to the exit without Laddie stopping along the way to greet a gray standard poodle and make a new friend. Laddie's wagging tail thumped the woman with the poodle, but she remained unperturbed, and we exchanged some idle chat about our dogs before I coaxed Laddie away from the poodle.

I drove to the park, where we began our walk. I checked the time on my phone every few minutes. I wanted to call the frame shop at ten, when it opened, and let someone, hopefully Brooks himself, know that I'd be stopping by to pick up my painting. It was highly unlikely that Melinda would try to claim it. She declared she'd never have it hanging in her house, but she was so angry with me, it wouldn't be beyond the realm of possibility that she might destroy it. I was probably letting my imagination run away with me, but I decided that it was prudent to take precautions, nevertheless.

On the stroke of ten, I called the frame shop while Laddie and I continued strolling through the park. I asked for Brooks, but, since he wasn't in, I told the clerk that my buyer had changed her mind about framing and that I'd be coming in to pick up my canvas later.

"Fine," she said. I got the feeling that she hadn't been paying close attention to what I said, and I realized I hadn't planned my trip very well. I should have left Laddie at home and been waiting outside the frame shop when it opened. Then, I could have dropped off the contract at the clinic later.

I turned to retrace our steps, and I hurried Laddie along. I couldn't take him into the Resort's mall, so I'd have to drop him off at home before I went to pick up my painting.

Laddie wouldn't be thrilled about staying home with Mona Lisa, but, as it turned out, he didn't have to. When Belle saw us returning, she invited him to come over to her house to play with Mr. Big.

"I won't be long, Belle," I promised.

"No worries. I'm planning on staying home the rest of the day. Take your time."

"Thanks." I was off with a wave to my friend. I'd certainly hit the jackpot when I'd moved next door to her and Dennis.

I didn't lose any time driving to the Resort. I pulled up under the canopy at the valet parking area near the entrance, handed my key to a valet, and took my parking stub. I'd have to tip the valet, but parking here would save me a long trek through the parking lot, balancing my bulky canvas, so I figured it would be well worth it.

The shops along the mall all boasted beautiful holiday displays in their windows, but I hurried past, intent on my mission.

A young woman I'd never seen before greeted me at the counter of the frame shop.

"Hi. I called earlier about picking up my painting. I'm not sure who I spoke to."

"Oh, yeah, I remember. That was me. Do you have your receipt?"

"Sure." I pulled my receipt out of my pocket and handed it to her.

"OK, Melinda," she said, handing the receipt back to me. "Your painting's in the back. I'll bring it out to you."

"Oh, no. I'm not Melinda. I'm Amanda Trent. See?" I pointed to the "received from" line on the receipt.

She frowned. "But it says Melinda Gibbs here." She indicated the instructions that stated Melinda Gibbs would be arranging for the framing. "I don't know about this."

"Look, I'm the artist. I dropped the painting off, and now I want to pick it up. Simple as that."

"But Mrs. Gibbs . . . . Isn't she the mayor?"

I was beginning to feel annoyed, but, rather than arguing with the confused clerk, I suggested she call Brooks.

"Oh, no. I couldn't do that. I'm not supposed to call him unless there's an emergency."

I had no such compunctions. I whipped my phone out and called Brooks myself. He'd given me his cell phone number a few months earlier, when he'd asked me for my help following an event we'd both participated in. Luckily, he answered. I'd been afraid my call might go to his voicemail, and, since I didn't seem to be getting anywhere with the clerk, I was depending on him to back me up. As soon as he answered, I launched into an explanation of my plight. He interrupted me after several seconds, telling me he'd "be right there."

"Brooks will be here in a little while," I told the clerk. We stood there and stared at each other for a minute before she returned to processing the paperwork she'd had on the counter when I arrived. I wandered around the shop, looking at examples of various frames.

Finally, Brooks arrived.

"Now, what's all this, Amanda?" he asked.

I pulled out my receipt and showed it to him. "I dropped one of my paintings off yesterday, but now I need to pick it up. Melinda Gibbs was going to buy it, but she changed her mind. It was here because she said she wanted to pick out a frame for it."

"No problem. Carol, would you please bring Ms. Trent's painting out?" He took the receipt, added a note that I'd picked up my painting, and initialed it with a flourish.

"Thanks, Brooks."

"Happy to help."

The clerk came out of the back room with my painting and set it on the counter.

"It's beautiful work, Amanda," Brooks said. "That's quite a large canvas to carry through the mall. Let me grab a dolly, and I'll wheel it out for you."

"That would be great. I parked in valet."

Brooks disappeared into the back room. Carol looked tense and avoided eye contact with me while I waited. I didn't really blame her for her reluctance to hand over my painting since she was just trying to do her job, so I thanked her for being careful.

She nodded and seemed to relax then.

Wheeling a dolly, Brooks came out of the back room and carefully placed my painting on it.

"It's a shame the mayor changed her mind," he said, as we walked through the mall, "but I'm sure someone else will buy it."

Such a transaction couldn't come soon enough, as far as I was concerned. Anyway, I was glad Brooks hadn't asked for details, and I decided to change the subject. "Our Roadrunner Christmas party certainly turned out differently than I'd expected. I still can't believe that girl thought it was a joke to bring a dessert that everybody in town associates with poison now."

"Yes, I thought it was odd, too. Alana, my office assistant, knows her family, and she told me that girl's always felt jealous of her sister, who, ironically, was one of the band members who was poisoned."

"Sounds as though it may have been a bid for attention. I hope she gets some help. You know, I thought she looked familiar when I saw her at the party. Now, I think I know why. I bet she looks a lot like her sister. I remember one of the band members bought something at our booth that day. I'll bet the buyer was the same girl who was poisoned. She and the others who survived the hemlock were the lucky ones, unlike poor Eric Thompson. Did you know him, by any chance?"

"No, I can't say that I did."

"The reason I asked is that you seemed to know his nephew Josh."

My comment was met by a bit of confusion from Brooks.

"At the Christmas party, he was with his girlfriend and Chip."

"Oh, right, but I had no idea who he was. I recognized him because I've seen him in my gallery. Well, here we are."

The wide doors to the Resort's entrance slid open, and we stopped at the valet station, where I handed a young man wearing the Resort's uniform my ticket stub. He grabbed my keys from a cabinet behind him and took off running. I noticed that most of the valets were young, probably because it took both speed and stamina to be able to do the job.

Brooks waited with me until the valet returned with my SUV. After he'd helped the valet secure my painting in the back, I thanked Brooks, handed the valet a tip, and drove off.

I didn't get too far before the receptionist from Dr. Madison's office called to let me know that he'd signed the paperwork, so I drove to the vet's office to pick it up, instead of going straight home.

The reception area wasn't nearly as packed as it had been earlier. There were only a couple of people waiting there with their dogs.

The receptionist saw me coming and handed me the contract as soon as I reached her desk. I gave it a cursory glance, saw his signature, folded it, and tucked it into my bag. When I looked up, I saw that Dr. Madison was standing behind the receptionist.

"Hi, Amanda. Do you have a minute?"

Chapter 32

"Yes, certainly."

"Let's go back to my office."

I followed him to the end of the short hallway and entered his tiny office. He didn't invite me to sit down, but picked up a stack of photos from his desk and handed them to me.

"Pictures of the pups," he said. "Katie asked me to give them to you. She noticed on your website that you work from photos."

"Great! These are very helpful, but I can do you one better since you live here in town. I like to see the pets I'll be painting in person, if possible. It gives me a good feel for their personalities, and I can also take a few pictures of my own. Would it be all right if I pay you a visit and see your dogs in action at home?"

"Oh, sure. Sounds like you really go the extra mile. Katie's going to be very impressed when I tell her. Would Sunday afternoon work for you?"

"That sounds fine. Say two o'clock?"

"Done." He scribbled his home address on the back of one of his business cards and handed it to me.

After I returned home, Belle and I enjoyed a quick lunch

before I headed to the Roadrunner.

As I drove downtown, I wondered whether any of the members of the Roadrunner had ever exhibited their art in a Scottsdale gallery. I felt sure that, if anyone had representation there now, I would have heard about it, but I made a mental note to ask Pamela.

I was still pondering that question when I arrived shortly before one. A few browsers were looking at paintings, and Pamela was talking to a woman at the jewelry counter while Ralph stood behind the cash register. I quickly stowed my coat and purse and joined Ralph.

"Busy day?" I asked.

"It's been fairly quiet so far. Maybe the big rush will come this afternoon," he joked.

The woman Pamela had been assisting at the jewelry counter left without making a purchase.

"I guess we can't win them all," Pamela said with a wry smile, after the prospective customer departed, "but Ralph, you've certainly had a good month."

"I've been lucky. It's feast or famine in this business." Ralph's phone chimed then, and he excused himself, walking a ways down the hall. He was back in a minute with a smile on his face.

"That was the mayor. She called to tell me how much she liked my painting that she bought for her husband's office."

I breathed a sigh of relief. At least Melinda's anger with me hadn't extended to another gallery member. Perhaps she'd even intended for me to find out that she'd called Ralph, although that notion was probably a stretch.

"That's fantastic, Ralph!" Pamela told him. "Amanda, wasn't Melinda interested in one of your paintings, too?"

At first, I was tempted to blurt out the whole story, but I thought better of it. "She decided against it."

"That's too bad," Pamela said sympathetically. She knew I was having a tough month. "By the way, I'm off this afternoon. Dawn's going to cover for me. I have to have a root canal, unfortunately. My mouth will be really numb, so I'm going to go home afterward."

A root canal didn't sound like anybody's idea of fun. We wished her well, and Dawn, accompanied by her mother Dorothy, arrived as Pamela was leaving.

"I'm off, too, now," Ralph announced. "See you ladies later."

After Dawn and Dorothy signed in, we all gathered near the counter. None of the browsers needed help, but we could keep an eye on the gallery and quickly respond if they did.

"Amanda, you were right to have concerns about the Christmas party. Never in the world would I have imagined that a high school choir member would try to frighten us all by putting carrot bars on the dessert table," Dorothy told me.

"She did a good job of disrupting the party; that's for sure," I said.

"I think Dave actually feels sorry for her. In his job, he sees a lot of kids who are in trouble, and that girl's so jealous of her sister that evidently she'll do anything to get attention. I guess it's not the first time she's done something inappropriate. It seems her sister's kind of a star—band leader, swim team, straight-A student, president of her class. It's a case of sibling rivalry gone too far," Dawn said.

"Well, I wish she hadn't decided to involve the Roadrunner. You can't tell me a girl that age doesn't know the difference between right and wrong. Sibling rivalry or not, her parents need to take her in hand."

Dorothy's last statement was so vehement that a few of our potential customers turned to see the source.

Dorothy clapped her hand over her mouth and muttered "sorry." Then, she strolled over to the customers who'd exhibited some curiosity and engaged them in conversation. Soon, they were looking at one of her elaborately embellished ceramic vases that was displayed on a pedestal and protected by a clear acrylic cover.

"Your mom has some strong opinions, doesn't she?"

"She does," Dawn chuckled. "She was so sure the Christmas party wouldn't present a problem. Of course, Dave would have to be the one cop on the spot at our party. Poor guy. He can't even go to an event without having to work. A week ago, we were at a basketball game at the high school when a fan got rowdy. He wouldn't quit, and Dave ended up having to arrest him. Last night, when we went out to dinner, he had to break up a fight in the parking lot."

"That's terrible. Whatever happened to the Christmas spirit?"

"I do wonder sometimes. Of course, I suppose a lot of people in Lonesome Valley feel on edge about those poisonings, especially since the case hasn't been solved yet."

"Saturday, the chief mentioned that a group of high school students might be involved."

"It turns out they're not. They've all been cleared, so Bill wants to start over, looking at all the evidence and leads."

"Sounds like Lieutenant Belmont. By the way, I noticed he was really chowing down at the reception after Eric Thompson's funeral Saturday afternoon. You'd think, after all he's been through with his heart attack and bypass surgery, he might change his diet. I'm afraid, if he keeps it up, he may have another heart attack."

"I know. I've talked to him about it until I'm blue in the face, but I never get anywhere. It's like he's oblivious."

"Denial, I suppose."

"You pegged it. He doesn't want to be thought of as weak or vulnerable. He's being awfully bullheaded, if you ask me."

"Frankly, I'm surprised that he's back at work already."

"Me, too. I know the chief wanted him to stay out on medical leave, but, since Bill's doctor cleared him to work, he's back at it." She glanced toward the gallery's front window. "Oh, speak of the devil. There's Bill now."

I turned around to look. Lieutenant Belmont was riding in the passenger seat of a patrol car stopped in traffic. I couldn't see who was driving, but chances were I wouldn't have known the officer, anyway. Mike Dyson had been the only patrol officer I was acquainted with, and he'd left Lonesome Valley for a job with the Phoenix Police Department a few months earlier.

I recognized the man in the back seat, though, and he did not look one bit happy as he glowered at the cops in the front seat.

Chapter 33

"That's Kevin Frazer in the back," I told Dawn.

"Who?"

"Eric Thompson's former partner. I saw him confront Eric outside that new restaurant on the highway about a week before Eric died, and they came to blows. Kevin claimed Eric owed him money, and he was furious that Eric had filed for bankruptcy."

"Is that the guy who tried to talk to Eric's nephew after the funeral? Dave told me there was an incident."

"Yes, he's the one." I watched as the police cruiser moved down the street and turned the corner.

"Could be he had something to do with the poisonings if he was that bent out of shape," Dawn speculated. "He sure didn't look too happy."

"That's the third time I've seen the man, and he's looked angry every time."

"Must have been a lot of money he was owed."

"And he definitely has a quick temper."

Several people came into the gallery then, and we split up to greet them and answer their questions. Out of the corner of my eye, I noticed that Dorothy was carefully lifting the clear top from the pedestal that held the ceramic vase. Later, I noticed that she had removed the vase and placed it on the counter. By the time Dawn and I finished talking to our prospective customers, the vase had gone home with its new owner.

"Nice sale," I told Dorothy.

"Thanks. We need something to replace it now. Dawn, you don't happen to have any pieces in the trunk, do you?"

"No, Mom, but it's not busy right now. I can run back to the studio and get one."

"How about that large platter you finished the other day—the one with the iridescent glaze? It's a stunner."

"All right. I'll be back shortly."

After Dawn left, I remembered that I'd intended to ask Pamela about whether any Roadrunner artists were represented by a gallery in Scottsdale. Pamela wasn't around, but Dorothy had been a member of the Roadrunner for years, and she knew everybody, so I decided to ask her.

"Galleries in Scottsdale? Let's see. I know Susan used to display her paper mâché animals in one of them, but you're probably more interested in our painters. Actually, I can't think of anybody who's represented there now."

"I wonder why Susan stopped."

"She said she couldn't keep up the pace. She likes to spend most of her time painting her watercolors. She could have hired some help to make more of her big paper mâché animals, but she wasn't interested in doing production work."

"Makes sense."

"Are *you* looking for gallery representation in Scottsdale?"

"I thought I'd check into it. Scottsdale has one of the best-known art districts in the Southwest, and it's only a two-hour drive from here."

"Well, I wish you luck. Dawn and I do fine with our ceramics business, but our Roadrunner sales wouldn't be enough to support us. Half our income comes from the classes we teach at our studio. You'd think there'd be a limit to the number of students in a small town like this, but we haven't found that to be the case. A lot of them buy a membership for open studio time, so they can work in our studio, rather than at home. We fire their work in our kilns, too, and give them storage space as well. Plus we sell the clay and glazes."

"I think that's fantastic." I'd visited their studio several months earlier, and I remembered being impressed with how organized they were.

"It works for us, but for an up-and-coming painter like you, displaying your artwork in a Scottsdale gallery would be just the ticket."

My talk with Dorothy bolstered my confidence, as did the fact that she thought of me as an "up-and-coming" artist. I knew seeking representation in Scottsdale wouldn't be easy, but, if I succeeded, I believed that it would be well worth the effort.

Half an hour later, Dawn returned with her large platter, which she carefully placed on the pedestal where her mother's vase had been displayed. She replaced the protective top and logged in her new piece in the gallery's inventory.

Dawn had returned in time to help with the sudden flood of customers, and we were busy the rest of the afternoon. I managed to sell one of my prints to a woman who admired my oil paintings but told me she couldn't afford an original. I suggested a print, instead, and, luckily, she liked the idea and found one that fit her budget.

Even though it wasn't a big sale, at least it was a sale, and it lifted my spirits. When we closed the gallery for the day, I drove home, feeling a bit more optimistic and determined not to let Melinda's canceled sale get me down.

After picking up Laddie at Belle's, I went home and gave my hungry pets their evening meal. Before preparing my own dinner, I turned on the TV to watch the local news. The anchor reported that there were no new developments in the investigation of the poisonings, and he asked that anyone with any information call the police department's special hotline. He noted that a reward was being offered for any information that led to the arrest of the crime's perpetrator. Finally, he added that there hadn't been any additional poisoning incidents since "local businessman Eric Thompson succumbed to hemlock poisoning last week."

Based on what Dawn had told me earlier, I hadn't really expected a break in the case. I wondered whether the chief's initial suggestion that an evil perpetrator who got a sick thrill from poisoning people and who might strike again had been spot on. I didn't know how likely that scenario was, considering that there had been just one source of the poisonings—so far, anyway.

After dinner, I removed my no-longer-sold painting from the back of my SUV and took it into the studio, hanging it in the same spot it had occupied before Melinda bought it.

Emma would be arriving Thursday, so I spent the rest of the evening searching art galleries for us to tour in Scottsdale, making notes about the type of artwork they featured, and paying special attention to application procedures. I knew better than to walk in off the street and pitch my artwork. Gallery owners seldom appreciated an artist's employing such a strategy, so I considered our tour of the galleries to be mainly a reconnaissance mission. Even if I didn't succeed in gaining representation at a Scottsdale art gallery, Emma and I would spend a fun day together, and I was looking forward to it.

Chapter 34

After walking Laddie the next morning, I buzzed around the house, cleaning and making sure everything was ready for Emma's arrival the next day. Sensing that something was up, Mona Lisa followed me. Laddie was normally the one to do that, but he hung back warily, letting Mona Lisa take over his routine.

During Emma's summer break, Mona Lisa had slept with her every night on the hide-a-bed in the living room. I had no doubt my finicky kitty would abandon me and Laddie for Emma again.

I was going through a stack of magazines, deciding which to keep and which to discard when Rebecca called. Although I often ran into her or Greg when I walked Laddie, I hadn't seen either of them since the reception.

"Amanda, I have a favor to ask," she said, after we exchanged greetings.

"Sure, What is it?" I asked, hoping she didn't need help the next day because I'd be in Phoenix to pick up Emma.

"Josh asked Greg and me to come over to Eric's house to select a memento before the auction house removes the contents. I think he feels bad that he had to borrow money for Eric's funeral from Greg, and he knows Eric himself owed Greg quite a bit of money. I'm guessing it was the only gesture he could think to offer right now. Anyway, Greg doesn't want to go, but I think I'd better put in an appearance, at least. I wouldn't want to hurt Josh's feelings, but I'd rather not go alone. I wonder if you'd come along with me."

"I can do that, depending on when you're planning to go."

"I was thinking sometime today, maybe even this morning, if it's convenient."

"That works for me."

"Say, in about an hour? I'll pick you up."

I had time to finish my magazine sorting task and tidy the studio before Rebecca arrived to pick me up. I didn't expect to be gone long, and I assured Laddie that I'd be back soon, before leaving him. Mona Lisa, seeing that I was about to depart, leaped to the top of her kitty tree and watched us from her perch.

"I feel a little bit strange about this," Rebecca confessed as she drove to Eric's place. "Looking through Eric's things—I don't know—seems kind of like an invasion of his privacy."

"Is that the reason Greg didn't want to come?"

"No. He has mixed feelings about Eric. I mean, he's sorry about what happened, and he felt obligated when Josh needed help paying for the funeral, but, at the same time, I know he's still furious that Eric never made any effort to pay him back."

"Maybe, if the lawsuit against the helicopter tour company pans out . . . ."

"I suppose so, but I'm not holding my breath. Josh told us all about it. What a weasel his lawyer turned out to be. He's going to look for a new attorney in Phoenix. And the mayor's husband—plain disgraceful. She won't ever be getting my vote again."

"Nor mine."

"Well, here we are."

Rebecca parked in the driveway at Eric's house.

"It looks like Josh isn't here yet, unless Kayla's dropped him off," I said.

"Oh, he isn't coming. He had to go back to work. His boss wasn't too happy that he took longer than a week's bereavement leave."

"Where does Josh work?" I realized nobody had ever mentioned his employment, although I'd assumed he had a job.

"At the Furniture Niche out on the highway. He's been there about a year, I think."

We got out of the car and walked up the steps to the porch. I waited for Rebecca to produce a key from her purse, but, instead, she lifted a flower pot with some greenery growing out of it that sat beside the front door and plucked a key from beneath it. I looked around to see if anybody was watching, and I caught a glimpse of a curtain fluttering next door at Sylvia Costa's house.

"Did Josh leave that key there?"

"No. He told me that's where Eric kept it."

"Hmm. Maybe you should give it to Josh when we're done. The neighbors could have noticed where you found the key. It's not a very secret hiding place."

"I suppose not," Rebecca said, unlocking the front door. We stepped inside, and Rebecca closed and locked it behind us.

"Let's go upstairs first," Rebecca suggested.

Before we started up the stairs, we heard a noise.

"What was that?" Rebecca whispered.

"I think it came from the kitchen." We looked at each other and froze as the bumping noise we heard was followed by footsteps. We weren't the only ones in the house! I reached into my purse for my phone, but, before I found it, we heard sirens and, seconds later, the back door slamming closed. Now that the intruder had departed, we hurried to the kitchen and looked out the large window above the sink, just in time to see a man run around the corner from the back, into the side yard, and collide with a uniformed officer. His partner quickly grabbed the fleeing man as the other officer scrambled to his feet and clapped handcuffs on the intruder who'd run into him.

One of the officers saw us watching from the window and motioned to us to come out. It wasn't until we were in the side yard that we had a good view of the man in cuffs. It was Kevin Frazer, and the last time I'd seen him, he'd been sitting in the back of a police car. Now, here he was, at Eric's house.

"Did one of you ladies call in a burglary report?" asked the officer Kevin had run into.

"No, we didn't," Rebecca said. "We came in the front door a few minutes ago, and we were about to go upstairs when we heard a noise in the kitchen. That was right before you got here."

In the commotion, we hadn't noticed Sylvia Costa come out, onto her side porch.

"I'm the one who called," she announced, startling us all. She pointed to Kevin. "I saw that man trying to get in the back door. Then, I heard glass breaking."

"You have anything to say for yourself?" the cop asked Kevin.

"I only want what's mine," he said sulkily, "and I'm not saying another word without my lawyer."

"You can contact your lawyer when we get to the station," the cop who'd handcuffed Kevin growled. "Terry, get the particulars, will you? I'm taking this guy to the car."

Officer Terry proceeded to take down our contact information and made some notes. He must have been on the scene the night Eric died, because he knew whose house had been burgled. We took him inside and walked around, but we weren't able to tell whether anything was missing. Then, we saw some papers strewn about, near Eric's desk, only a few feet from where he'd died. Other than that, nothing seemed to be amiss downstairs.

Upstairs, we peeked into a couple of small, spartan bedrooms. The much-larger and well-furnished master bedroom at the end of the hallway featured an en suite bathroom and a walk-in closet. The covers on the king-size bed were rumpled, as though someone had just gotten out of bed. On the last day of his life, Eric would never have imagined he wouldn't be returning to sleep there.

"Oh!" Rebecca exclaimed when she opened the closet door. "Natalie's clothes are still here. It doesn't look as though Eric ever got rid of any of them after she died."

She backed out of the closet and went to a carved wooden jewelry box that sat on the dresser in the master bedroom.

"This is empty," she told Terry after she'd checked it, "but Eric may have given away or sold his wife's jewelry after she died. She did have a couple of antique pieces, but mostly she wore costume jewelry, which wouldn't be valuable."

We trooped back downstairs, and Terry paused in the living room to answer a call from his partner.

"You mentioned antique jewelry," he said to Rebecca. "Can you describe it?"

"There was a long rope necklace of real pearls and an art deco diamond and platinum ring. Natalie inherited them from her great-grandmother, along with this house."

"Did your partner find them?" I asked.

"Our burglar did. They were stuffed in his jacket pocket. I don't think his lawyer's going to be able to get him out of this one, like he did yesterday."

"I can't believe Kevin stooped so low, and to think he and Eric used to be friends," Rebecca said.

"We'll be in touch," Terry said. "Someone will need to identify the jewelry. Are you the executor of the estate?" he asked Rebecca.

"No, just a relative. Eric's nephew, Josh Thompson, is the executor. I can give you his phone number."

Terry jotted it down with his other notes. "Does he drive a red sports car?"

"Yes, he does," I volunteered.

"I remember him."

He left it at that. Since Terry had been one of the officers called out when Eric died, he'd probably witnessed how upset Josh had been that night.

"Better get that back window repaired right away," he suggested on his way out. "Somebody else might try to get in."

"I'll take care of it," Rebecca assured him, and she called Greg the minute he left.

"I know you didn't want to come over to Eric's," Rebecca told her husband, "but I'm afraid we're going to need some help."

When she finished talking, she said, "He'll be right over with some plywood to board up the window until Josh can get it repaired. He certainly has his hands full with everything that's happened. And now this."

Chapter 35

While we waited for Greg to arrive, Rebecca and I picked up the papers that Kevin had dumped on the floor in Eric's office. On glancing at them, we could see that they contained nothing of interest to him. Instead, most of them were unpaid bills. I speculated that he'd become frustrated and tossed them aside.

We stacked the bills neatly on the corner of the desk for Josh to retrieve before the auction house personnel came to remove the furniture and other household goods.

"I still haven't picked out a memento," Rebecca said. Suddenly, she smiled. "I have it. I remember Natalie had that painting I liked—a desert scene with mountains in the background. It used to be above the sofa in the living room. I don't remember seeing it there today, though."

"Why don't we double check?"

"Yes, let's. It would look nice in our den, I think."

In the living room, a framed print hung above the sofa.

"Not there. Come to think of it, it's probably been a while since I've seen it. Oh, well. I'll settle for those brass bookends I saw in the office and call it a day." She glanced out the front window. "Here comes Greg now."

We went outside, and Rebecca helped Greg carry the

plywood while I grabbed the hammer and box of nails he'd brought and followed them around back.

It didn't take Greg long to secure the plywood over the broken window.

"That ought to do it," he said, as he hammered the last nail in place. "Josh isn't going to be happy about this, especially when he hears who did it. Kevin's gone beyond a nuisance, breaking and entering and stealing Natalie's jewelry. I don't know what's wrong with that guy."

"He's certainly persistent, in a bad way," I said.

"Not much more we can do here," Rebecca observed. "Are you sure you don't want to come in and look around?"

"I'm sure."

"OK. I'll just grab those brass bookends and lock up. See you at home in a few minutes."

After Rebecca retrieved the bookends and locked the front door, I had an idea.

"Rebecca, let's go next door for a minute and thank Sylvia for calling the police."

"All right."

Before we started up her steps, Sylvia came out, onto the front porch.

"Hello, Amanda."

"Hi, Sylvia. This is my friend, Rebecca Winters. She's one of Eric's relatives. We just want to thank you for calling the police. We'll never know what Kevin would have done if he'd found us in the house."

"It was obvious the man was up to no good. You know him?"

"I know who he is. He was Kevin's former partner."

"Ah. That explains it. He looked somewhat familiar. I must

have seen him next door at one time or another, but not lately."

"You haven't noticed anybody else hanging around the house, have you?"

"Only Jack, but he let himself in with the key."

"You mean the key Eric left under the flower pot?"

"Right. I figure if he knew where to get it, he was probably checking on something for Josh."

"Come on, Amanda; we'd better get going," Rebecca said, as she tugged at my sleeve.

I nodded and waved goodbye to Sylvia. As we were walking to Rebecca's car, I asked, "What's wrong, Rebecca? You didn't say a word to Sylvia."

"I know. I was so dumbstruck by her brooch that I didn't know what to say."

"The huge red poinsettia pin?"

"The last time I saw it, Natalie was wearing it. I'm sure it's the same brooch."

"You think Sylvia stole it?"

"She knew where Eric kept the key."

"Could Natalie have given the brooch to Sylvia, perhaps as a Christmas present?"

"I suppose it's possible, but it's also possible that she helped herself to it."

"Sylvia doesn't strike me as a thief, but I don't really know her all that well."

We hopped into the car, and Rebecca backed out of the driveway.

"You're definitely right about returning the house key to Josh. I'll make sure he gets it today. It seems as though anybody in the neighborhood might know about it, not only Sylvia and Jack. The funny thing is that, when I told Greg about it, he acted as though he didn't even hear me. Normally, something like a house key being kept outside, where people can find it, would really set him off. You know how obsessed he is with personal safety and protecting property. Maybe Eric's death hit him harder than I realized, but he doesn't even seem that concerned with any news about the poisonings."

I had to admit Greg's attitude didn't sound like the Greg I knew. As Rebecca said, he'd always been security conscious.

"Maybe you should ask him about it."

"You're right. I'm going to mention this key business when I get home and see how he reacts this time."

As soon as Rebecca dropped me off, my pets scrambled to greet me. They were both ready for some playtime, so I obliged them before having my lunch and looking over the menu I'd made for this evening's meal.

I'd invited Belle and Dennis to dinner this particular night because I wanted to give them their Christmas present before they left for their trip to Michigan on Saturday. Knowing I'd be busy picking Emma up the next day and occupied Friday with my studio tour in the evening, I'd decided this was the best time to do it.

Glancing at the menu I'd jotted down, I decided not to make any changes. It was a hearty meal, appropriate for a cold winter day—stuffed pork chops, baked apples, garlic mashed potatoes, green beans, and pecan pie for dessert. The pie was the only menu item I could prepare ahead of time, so I made it before spending some time in my studio.

As I painted, I thought about Eric's untimely demise. Because of his impending bankruptcy, all his creditors had reason to be angry with him, although his ex-partner certainly had been the most vocal. Bob Gibbs wouldn't have minded if

Eric's lawsuit went away. Could he have thought that Eric's death would end it, only to find out later that Josh intended to continue to pursue litigation?

Everything seemed to center around Eric, and his house had become a point of interest, too, not only to Kevin Frazer, but also to Eric's neighbors.

There were more questions than answers. I wondered what had happened to Natalie's costume jewelry as well as the painting Rebecca had wanted and why Eric hadn't sold the valuable pearls and diamond ring, which, I felt certain, would bring several thousand dollars, if sold. I also wondered whether Josh had any idea of the value of the two pieces of antique jewelry, which surely would command a much higher price at a specialty auction, rather than a local auction featuring mainly furniture and household goods.

I made a mental note to alert Josh, although I felt a bit awkward about doing so. He'd felt grateful that I'd clued him in about the bribe the mayor's husband had offered Josh's lawyer, yet I remembered an impression I'd had at the time that he'd thought of me as a busybody. Now, here I was again, poking my nose into his business. I decided to tell Chip, instead, and ask him to pass the information along to his friend. By now, the police would have informed Josh about the burglary at his uncle's house, but that didn't mean he knew how valuable the stolen necklace and ring were.

As soon as I put my paints away and moved the canvas I'd been working on to the corner of the studio, I called Chip to ask him to tell Josh about the value of the stolen jewelry.

"All right, Amanda, I'll wait until he brings up the burglary, and then I'll suggest he check into selling the antique pieces elsewhere. I won't even mention your name, if you don't want me to."

"Thanks, Chip. That would be fine."

"No problem."

With that task taken care of, I went to the studio closet and brought out my painting of Mr. Big. I placed it on an easel squarely in the center of the studio, facing the door to the living room.

Then, I stood back and admired my work. The little dog looked absolutely adorable.

I smiled as I turned off the lights and pulled the door closed so that Belle and Dennis wouldn't see their Christmas present until the big reveal after dinner.

Chapter 36

"Merry Christmas!" Belle said as she handed me a silver wrapped flat package with a huge red bow on top.

"Merry Christmas to you, too!"

Mr. Big strained at his leash, and Belle stooped to unsnap it from his collar while Dennis followed her into the kitchen, carrying their card table. I'd asked to borrow it for our dinner because my little two-seater table literally did not have room for more than two people.

Laddie and Mr. Big jumped and ran around until I corralled them in a corner so that Dennis could set up the card table.

"All set," he said. "I'm going to take these two outside until you're ready." He called the dogs and headed for the back door.

"Thanks, Dennis."

With our canine companions happily occupied and out from underfoot, Belle set the table while I finished preparing the garlic mashed potatoes and warming the green beans. I'd timed the pork chops and the baked apples to be done in a few minutes.

When all the food was ready to be served, Belle called Dennis. The dogs rushed back into the house and came straight to the kitchen. I set a bowl down for Mr. Big, next to Laddie's dish, and put a couple of treats in each, tiny ones for Mr. Big and larger ones for Laddie. It took only seconds for them to devour their snacks, but they were satisfied, and when we told them to lie down as soon as we began eating dinner, they complied. Mona Lisa had ducked into the bedroom as soon as Mr. Big made his appearance, and she wasn't about to come out any time soon.

"Are you sure you wouldn't like to have your Christmas dinner at our house?" Belle asked. Of course, Belle and Dennis's spacious house had far more room than mine did, including a large kitchen and a separate dining room, so it was a practical suggestion as well as a generous one.

"Thanks, Belle, but I think I'd rather have it here. You know, my first Christmas in my very own home. I know it's small, but—"

"It's cozy."

I smiled. "Yes, exactly, and I do appreciate your inviting Dustin and my parents to stay at your house while they're visiting. It'll be so much handier than if they had to book motel rooms."

"We're happy to do it, Amanda," Dennis said. "By the way, Emma texted me earlier today. She said she'd like to come in for work at the feed store, starting Friday."

"Really? I thought she'd want to wait until Monday."

"I think a certain young man who works at the feed store might have something to do with it."

"Hmm. Emma never mentioned anyone."

"Maybe I shouldn't have, either. I noticed last summer that they were friendly."

"It's news to me, but she hasn't been dating anyone at college. I can't wait to see her."

"Bring Laddie over as early as you need to in the morning. I know you'll be wanting to get to the airport a little early. Dennis will be up, won't you, honey?"

"I sure will. I never could sleep in. Not like some people I know." He grinned and rolled his eyes in Belle's direction.

We cleared the dishes, and Dennis folded the card table.

"Where would you like me to put the table?" he asked. It was staying until after my parents and Dustin went home. "How about the studio?"

"Wait a second. Could you just leave it behind the sofa for now? I'd like to give you your Christmas present, and it's in the studio." I opened the door and switched the light on.

Belle rushed forward and gazed at Mr. Big's portrait. She drew in a sharp breath. "Oh, Amanda, it's wonderful! You've really captured Mr. Big's personality!" She hugged me. "Thank you so much!"

"I don't know how you do it, Amanda," Dennis said. "He looks exactly like the little scamp he is."

"I know just where I want to hang it," Belle said. "I can't thank you enough. It's such a perfect gift."

"I'm glad you like it."

"We love it, and we have a gift for you, too. Why don't you open it now?" Belle urged, as she picked up my gift that I'd left sitting on an end table, next to the sofa, and gave it to me.

I tore off the bow and the silver wrapping paper, revealing a flat white box. I lifted the cover and removed the contents—a paper with a schematic drawing on it. Confused, I looked at Belle and Dennis.

"Turn it over," Belle urged.

On the back was written, "Your new garage."

"We're going to convert your carport into a garage," Dennis

explained, "complete with automatic door."

I felt so stunned by their gift, which was both thoughtful and practical, that I was almost speechless.

"Well, what do you think?" Belle asked.

"It's wonderful! I'm sorry I'm tongue-tied. It's such a surprise."

"Good; for a minute there, I was afraid you didn't like it," Belle said.

"Oh, no. I love it. I'm just blown away; that's all," I assured her.

Dennis and Belle grinned at each other.

"Now, there's just one more detail, and we're all set," Dennis said. "We need to get a building permit from the city. All you have to do is sign the application, and, as soon as the city issues the permit, we're in business."

Belle pulled the document from her purse and handed it to me.

I quickly scribbled my name on the dotted line and gave it back to her.

"I'm still trying to wrap my mind around having a real garage. It'll be so much handier, and I'll actually be able to store stuff in there without worrying that it might disappear."

"It's not as big a project as it seems at first. You already have three walls and a roof, so all we have to build is the front and then install the door."

"That sounds like plenty to me."

"I think we can get it done in a day. Brian's volunteered to help with the construction."

"That's nice of him. He mentioned to me once that it would be a good idea to enclose my carport, but that was months ago. He never gave me a hint about what you were planning."

"I think he's a keeper, Amanda," Belle said with a wink. "But no pressure." She held up her hand as I started to reply.

"All right, Mrs. Cupid. I'll keep that in mind."

We chatted for a while longer, and, when Belle and Dennis left, she assured me that Mr. Big's portrait would be in its place soon and I could see it there when I dropped off Laddie in the morning.

After they left, I returned to the kitchen to load the dishwasher. I'd just turned it on when my phone rang. I half-expected to see Brian's name pop up on the caller ID, but the call came from Rebecca.

"Hi, Amanda. I hope I'm not calling too late."

"Not at all. It's only nine o'clock. What's up?"

"A couple of things. Remember when I said I was going to talk to Greg?"

"Sure."

"Well, I did, and he denied anything was wrong. He said he was just a little preoccupied."

"With the poisonings and Eric's death?"

"So he said, and he sounded reasonable, but I got to thinking about it, and that doesn't make any sense. If that's what's on his mind, he would have been way more concerned about the break-in, but he acted almost nonchalant. I don't know what to think. He took Skippy and Tucker to the park, so I thought I'd give you a call while he was out."

"I'm afraid I'm stumped. Is there something else that could be worrying him?"

"If there is, he hasn't mentioned it to me. He just doesn't seem like himself. It's a little weird."

Although I could understand her point, I didn't really have any sage advice to offer. "I wish I knew what to tell you."

"That's OK. I just needed to talk to someone who doesn't think I'm imagining things."

"You're not imagining things," I assured her.

"Maybe he'll open up later. I probably shouldn't push him."

"That might be the best idea," I agreed. "You mentioned there was something else."

"Oh, right. I was thinking about the painting I was going to keep as a memento but then it wasn't there. What if someone stole that, too? I think a lot of people knew where that key was stashed."

"Evidently. But why that particular picture? It doesn't seem like an item that would attract a thief."

"Yes, I guess that's true, but I think it was an antique, too, because it was in the house when Natalie inherited it."

"Antique paintings aren't necessarily valuable, though. Age alone doesn't determine desirability in the art world. It really depends on the reputation of the painter and the condition of the work. Unless a well-known artist painted it, it's probably not worth too much."

"I guess you're right. From what I remember Natalie telling me, some local guy painted it and gave it to Natalie's great-grandparents way back in the day. I was thinking about going back to the house and looking for it in the attic, but I guess I won't bother. I mentioned that I couldn't find it to Josh, and he shrugged it off. He didn't even remember the painting, but he said I was welcome to search the attic if I wanted to. I told him I'd let him know, but, now that I've talked to you, I think I'll drop it. I don't especially feel like rummaging around in a dusty attic."

"I imagine the auction house will remove anything from the attic, too. You could always check to see if the painting ends up in the auction, if you really want it."

"It's not that I want it so much. It's that I think someone may have walked off with it, and, if it was valuable, the proceeds from selling it should go to Eric's estate. That's why I thought I should tell Josh, but he wasn't interested."

"If the estate's so deeply in debt, maybe he figures he wouldn't get any of the money, anyway."

"That's true enough. Eric didn't do him any favor when he named Josh executor. It's already been a lot of work for Josh, and it's not over yet. His only hope of getting anything from the estate would be that lawsuit and, so far, he hasn't found an attorney in Phoenix who's willing to take the case. It would have to be on contingency, of course."

"Right. Otherwise, Josh would have to pay the lawyer's fee up front."

"And he can't afford. . . ." Rebecca stopped talking mid-sentence. "Oops, I better go now. I hear Greg and the pups coming in. Have a safe trip tomorrow and have fun with your daughter in Scottsdale."

Chapter 37

The next morning, when the raucous blast of my alarm clock woke me, I felt a knot in my stomach, probably due to a combination of the early hour and my excitement at the prospect of Emma's arrival. Mona Lisa opened her eyes and closed them again as soon as I shut off the alarm. She didn't make a move to get out of bed. Laddie, on the other hand, was raring to go, almost as if he sensed he'd be spending the day with his little buddy.

The first thing I did was check on Emma's flight to confirm that it wouldn't be delayed. It was scheduled to depart on time, but the flight, from Los Angeles to Phoenix, would take less time than the drive from Lonesome Valley to the Sky Harbor Airport, so I'd have to leave before I knew for sure that Emma's flight was in the air.

I rushed through my morning routine and dropped Laddie off with Dennis before I got on the road. It was still dark outside. The sun wouldn't be up for an hour and a half, and it felt slightly spooky since I was the only customer at the pumps after I pulled into the deserted gas station on the outskirts of town to fill up. I tapped my credit card on the reader next to the gas pump, but nothing happened. After a couple more unsuccessful tries, I had to go inside the station to pay. I wondered whether I'd miscalculated and gone over my credit card limit, especially when the clerk had a problem with the card, too. Just when I was about to offer cash instead, he finally succeeded in running the transaction.

"Sorry about that," he said, as he handed my card back. "You're good to go."

"Thanks," I said, as I hurried out the door. The stop for gas was taking a little longer than I'd anticipated, but I'd still be at the airport by the time Emma's flight landed. While I waited for the tank to fill, I checked my phone for the flight status and felt happy that it hadn't changed.

Finally, I was on my way. Traffic was light on the highway that led to Interstate 17, but the traffic increased as I drove through central Phoenix, jumped onto Interstate 10, and exited at the airport. I found a parking spot in one of the cell phone lots. I checked the information display for Emma's flight and found that my timing had been perfect. Her flight had just arrived.

It wasn't long before Emma called me, and I proceeded to the crowded curb area to pick her up. She wore a backpack over a light jacket, jeans, and sneakers, and her dark, wavy hair was shorter than it had been in the summer. With all the traffic around us, I didn't dare get out of the car. I popped the back door so she could stow her suitcase before she eased into the passenger seat beside me. We managed a quick hug before the driver behind me started honking, so I pulled out of my curbside spot, and we were soon on our way to Scottsdale.

"Hungry?" I asked as we drove north.

"Starving. I had some juice on the plane, but that's it."

"I only had a piece of toast when I got up, so I'm ready for a nice brunch this morning. My friends at the Roadrunner suggested a couple of restaurants in Old Town Scottsdale; that's right where the galleries are. Oh, and the boutiques, too."

"Sounds good to me."

We stopped at the first place on my list and enjoyed a leisurely brunch while Emma told me about her finals.

"When are Grandma and Gramps going to get here?" she asked.

"Monday, and Dustin's flying in then, too. They've coordinated their arrivals, so that they arrive about the same time. Dustin reserved a rental car, so they can all drive to Lonesome Valley together."

"I can't wait to see them," she said. "This is going to be a way better Christmas than last year."

"I know. Last year was sad for all of us. I'm sorry."

"It's not your fault, Mom," Emma said. "Dad's the one to blame. When I visited him at Thanksgiving, I felt like a stranger in our house."

"And I don't even have a bedroom for you," I lamented.

"Oh, I didn't mean that. I like your house. It's cute and comfy."

"Are you sure you don't mind sleeping on the hide-a-bed?"

"Not at all." Emma sighed. "I know I have to get used to the new normal, but I'm not there yet."

"Well, give it time. I know that sounds terribly trite, but I don't know what else to say."

"Yeah, I know. It just gets to me sometimes."

"Would another cinnamon roll help?" I asked, as I slid the basket of pastries toward my daughter.

"It wouldn't hurt," Emma said with a grin, as she helped herself.

Happy that her mood had brightened, I showed her the map

of Old Town Scottsdale and pointed out some of the galleries and boutiques that we might visit.

I drank a second cup of coffee while Emma finished her roll, and then we headed toward the shops. Emma bought some earrings and a cute top, and I bought her a pair of boots, which, luckily for my pocketbook, had been marked down considerably.

After spending a couple hours shopping, we headed to the art galleries on East Main Street. I enjoyed seeing the variety of artworks as we browsed through several galleries before we came to the first one that I'd flagged as a potential venue for my own artwork. As soon as we entered, I knew that my paintings would fit right in, but after the gallery's owner approached us and kept up a very aggressive patter of sales talk the entire time we were there, I decided the place wasn't for me.

Once we left, Emma said, "Talk about obnoxious."

"I agree. I wouldn't want to be represented by that gallery. Let's try the next."

The second gallery on my list of possibilities didn't appeal to me, either, although, again, I thought my artwork would have been a good fit. This time, we were totally ignored by the gallery's staff, so I scratched that one off my list, too.

"This might be harder than I thought," I told Emma when we were outside on the sidewalk. "Everybody in all the galleries has been great, except the last two, not so much." Consulting my list, I said, "It looks like the next one is about a block from here, around the corner."

The minute we walked in, I had a good feeling. The place was airy and full of light, and the sales staff were friendly but not obtrusive.

"I think I'll apply to this one," I whispered to Emma as we browsed the paintings.

"You totally should," Emma agreed.

I took one of my brochures out of my bag to show Emma which paintings I planned to submit images of with my application to the gallery, but it slipped from my hand and fluttered to the floor. Before I could retrieve it, a bearded young man wearing a sports coat scooped it up. I thought he was about to hand it back to me before he glanced at it, but then he stopped to look it over.

"Are you Amanda Trent?" he asked.

My name, but not my photo, appeared on the front of the brochure.

"Yes, I am."

"May I?" he asked, unfolding it to look inside.

"Of course."

After he'd studied the brochure for a few minutes, he gave it back to me and stuck out his hand while introducing himself as Ian Adams. I recognized his name immediately since the gallery bore the same name. After I introduced him to Emma, he shook hands with her, too, before turning to me.

"I noticed you're represented by the Crystal Star Gallery in Kansas City. I'm familiar with it. Are you looking for representation here in Scottsdale?"

"I am, as a matter of fact. I'm planning to fill out your application form."

"That's fine, and I'll keep it on file, but, from the images I've seen in your brochure, I believe that I may be able to take you on as a featured artist. I'd need to see your original work first, of course. Would tomorrow be convenient?"

"I could arrange that if I could come by in the morning. I live in Lonesome Valley, so it's a two-hour drive, and I have a studio tour in the evening."

"How about ten o'clock, right when we open?"

"That would be fine."

"If you'd bring ten representative works, I'd appreciate it."

"Yes, I will," I said, and we exchanged business cards. I managed to contain my excitement, but it wasn't easy!

Finally, after Emma and I left the gallery and crossed the street, we hugged each other, and I let out a whoop of joy.

"I think I'm looking at the newest featured artist at the Ian Adams Gallery," Emma said. "Way to go, Mom!"

Chapter 38

Passersby gave us some sidelong glances, since I was practically jumping up and down with joy until a warning thought crossed my mind. Perhaps I shouldn't get too excited yet. Melinda's cancellation of my big sale to her had happened only a few days earlier. Even though Ian Adams had expressed interest in my paintings, there was no guarantee that he'd decide to take me on as a featured artist in his gallery.

Emma noticed right away that I'd quieted down. "What's wrong, Mom?"

"What if Ian decides he doesn't want to show my paintings?"

"What if he does? Come on, Mom. Get a grip. He wouldn't have asked you to bring them if he wasn't really interested."

"I suppose so."

"Don't worry. He's going to sign you up. I just know it."

"I hope so. I'd love to be represented by a gallery here in Scottsdale, and Ian's seems perfect for my artwork."

We stopped at a couple more galleries on the way back to the car, but nothing I saw in either of them registered with me. I was too busy thinking about tomorrow's trip back to Scottsdale and hoping it would end with an agreement to exhibit my paintings in Ian's gallery.

"Would you like to stop someplace on the way home for a late lunch?" I asked Emma when we reached the car.

"Let's go back to Lonesome Valley and have an early dinner at home," Emma suggested. "I can't wait to see Mona Lisa and Laddie."

We went straight to Belle's to pick up Laddie as soon as we got back to Lonesome Valley. My golden boy pranced with excitement at seeing Emma, and he ran back and forth, from me to Emma and back again with Mr. Big trailing behind and barking all the way.

An equally warm reception from Mona Lisa awaited Emma at home. My little calico cat wasted no time in snuggling up to my daughter. She meowed loudly and wrapped herself around her ankles the second we entered the house. She refused to quiet down until Emma picked her up for a cuddle, and she protested loudly when she put her back down.

Emma sat on the sofa and called Mona Lisa to her. My kitty settled in her lap, purring happily.

"Looks as though she missed you," I commented.

"For sure, and I missed her, too, didn't I, Mona Lisa?"

Mona Lisa purred more loudly, as if to agree with Emma.

"I think I'm trapped for a while."

"You just relax. I'm going to put your suitcase in the bedroom, and you can unpack later. The closet's a bit crowded, but there's enough room to hang your clothes, and I've left the dresser drawers that you used last summer empty, so you can put anything that doesn't need to be hung up in those."

"Great. I'll unpack in a little while. Mona Lisa can help, can't you, baby?"

"Purr" came the answer.

I'd made plenty of food for my dinner with Belle and

Dennis the previous evening so that I'd have enough left over for Emma and me. I warmed everything in the oven while Emma played with Mona Lisa and petted Laddie, drawing a protest from Mona Lisa, who batted her arm every time she stroked Laddie's soft fur.

After dinner, we both proclaimed that we felt stuffed following our big brunch and substantial dinner, so we opted to skip dessert and save our chocolate meringue pie for later.

Emma had arranged to ride with Dennis to work the next day, and Belle had volunteered to watch Laddie again while I made another trip to Scottsdale, so, with our arrangements made, I headed to the studio to select the paintings to show Ian Adams the next day. While I hadn't expected to be making a second trip to Scottsdale, I was happy to do it, given the possibility that I might obtain representation at Ian's gallery.

The walls in my studio looked a bit empty when I'd finished removing the paintings I'd chosen to take with me. Emma helped me rearrange the remaining paintings, making sure there was more space between them. When we were done, the studio looked just fine, and the extra space between the paintings made each artwork stand out.

"Shall we load these into the car tonight or in the morning?" Emma asked.

"Let's do it in the morning. I won't have a real garage for a while."

"OK," Emma said with a yawn.

We'd both gotten up early, so we decided to call it a night. We pulled out the hide-a-bed and arranged the bedding. Mona Lisa jumped up on it, to spend the night with Emma, so I brought out her favorite pillow from my bed. She immediately curled up on it. Laddie didn't mind his feline companion's fickleness in abandoning us in favor of Emma, now that he could have me to himself.

I was so excited at the prospect of showing my artwork at Ian's gallery that I thought I might not be able to sleep, but that didn't prove to be the case, and I dropped off to the sound of Laddie's soft, rhythmic breathing a few minutes after I crawled into bed.

In the morning, after a quick breakfast, Emma and I loaded the paintings into the back of my SUV. There was no time to take Laddie for a walk, but I knew he'd have fun with Mr. Big, and, if I got home in time, we could go for a stroll in the afternoon. We all departed about the same time, with Dennis and Emma headed to work at the feed store while Belle, still dressed in her robe, stood in her doorway, holding Mr. Big, with Laddie by her side, and waved goodbye to us.

On the way to Scottsdale, the miles seemed to go by faster than they had yesterday, perhaps because I was listening to an audiobook about art marketing. When I arrived in Scottsdale, I found a parking spot around the corner from the Ian Adams Gallery. I was just a few minutes early, so the gallery would be opening soon. There was no way I could carry ten oil paintings, so I grabbed two that weren't bulky and walked around the corner to the gallery. Ian himself was unlocking the door when I arrived, and he sent a clerk with a dolly back to my car to collect the other paintings I'd brought to show him. He looked each of them over very carefully, but his bland expression never changed, and I didn't have a clue about what he was thinking. In fact, I was beginning to feel nervous about his lack of reaction, but then he turned to me and spoke for the first time since the clerk had returned with my paintings.

"Welcome to my gallery!"

The rest of our conversation was a blur. By the time I departed, leaving all ten paintings with Ian, I realized we'd discussed pricing and our agreement as well as other business details and even the future possibility of a solo show. I couldn't have been happier. Even though the commission the gallery would earn on a sale was steeper than at the Roadrunner, it was worth it for the exposure of my work in a gallery right in the heart of Old Town Scottsdale's art district.

The day before, Emma and I had approached the gallery from the opposite direction, but we'd never made it to the block where I was now parked. I looked around for a restaurant so that I could get a cup of coffee and maybe a croissant before driving back to Lonesome Valley. I could see a menu board on the sidewalk a few doors down, so I walked on past my car, but, before I reached the cafe, something else caught my eye.

I'd been idly gazing in the windows as I walked by the galleries, and I spotted a painting on an easel in the window of the auction house I was passing. I stopped for a closer look because the painting was of a desert scene with mountains in the background, just as Rebecca had described the picture she was looking for at Eric's house.

Of course, there were probably thousands of paintings in existence that could fit her description, but, out of curiosity, I decided to go inside and inquire about it. I didn't get very far, though. Evidently, the auction house was open to the public only for previews and live auctions. A sign on the door referred prospective customers to the auction's website, where they could view images of the artworks for sale and download auction catalogs.

On a whim, I took a few pictures of the painting with my cell phone camera, although taking them through the window wasn't ideal. I changed angles several times to avoid the glare off the plate glass window, before going on to the cafe, which didn't have any croissants but did have tempting apple strudel displayed in a glass case next to the front door.

I took a seat at one of the tables scattered around the small room and ordered a strudel and coffee when a server came to take my order. The strudel was so delicious I was tempted to order a second piece, but I restrained myself. There would be plenty more holiday goodies in the next week.

While I sipped my coffee, I looked at the pictures I'd taken. Only a couple of them had turned out fairly well. Even so, although the artist's signature appeared at the bottom right of the desert-and-mountains painting, I couldn't make it out.

After that, I searched the auction house's website to see if I could find the painting listed there. The house had several auctions scheduled, and, if I'd had to search all the catalogs for the painting, it would have taken forever, but I lucked out, since I found it displayed as a featured image on the homepage. I clicked a link and was taken to a page with a description of the painting, which was simply titled "Desert at Dawn," and a short biography of the artist, Miles Milford.

The name sounded vaguely familiar. I'd probably heard of him in one of my art history classes in college, although, admittedly, I'd paid far more attention to what my professors said in my studio art classes than in art history.

I scanned the bio, and I knew I'd made a connection when I read that Miles Milford had lived in Lonesome Valley, Arizona, in the years following World War II, before moving to Southern California, where he lived the rest of his life.

"Desert at Dawn," painted by an artist who'd lived in Lonesome Valley decades ago: this painting had to be the one

Rebecca had wanted, the same painting that had disappeared from Eric's house. With all the people who had access to the house because they knew where Eric had kept his key, it was impossible to guess who had taken it. Only the auction house staff knew who was offering the painting for sale. Somehow, I had to find out, but I doubted very much that the auction house's management would be willing to share that information. Perhaps a police inquiry would persuade them. As I put a tip on the table for my server, I decided it just might be time to give Lieutenant Belmont a call.

Chapter 39

Before I called the lieutenant, I decided I should confirm that "Desert at Dawn" was indeed the painting Rebecca had told me about. Once I got back to my car, I texted her the photo I'd taken of the Miles Milford work, along with a brief note asking whether she recognized it. When she didn't answer right away, I decided to get on the road, but, before I started the car, I made a last-ditch effort to contact someone at the auction house. It wasn't much of a surprise that nobody answered; after all, the place was closed. When I was prompted to leave a message, I decided against it. Perhaps the auction house was closed for the holidays. I hadn't really paid attention to the dates of scheduled auctions, so I brought up their website on my phone again and learned that no auctions were scheduled until after New Year's. For all I knew, the owners could be in Hawaii right now, and I surmised it would prove difficult, even for the police, to ferret out more information in the next ten days, at least, when many small businesses took an annual holiday break.

I still hadn't heard from Rebecca, so I began to drive back to Lonesome Valley. I was so preoccupied with trying to figure out the various ways the painting could have ended up at the auction house in Scottsdale that I didn't listen to my audiobook on the way home.

Just as I reached the outskirts of Lonesome Valley, my phone beeped. I pulled over to the side of the road, anticipating a response from Rebecca, and I had one. The message, punctuated by lots of exclamation marks, confirmed my suspicion that the painting was the very same one that used to hang in Eric's house.

I decided to call her before I mentioned it to Lieutenant Belmont, but, first, I wanted to pick up Laddie from Belle's. She'd need some time to finish packing for herself and Dennis before they left on their trip tomorrow, and watching two active dogs might delay her progress.

Belle was doing laundry when I arrived, and she took me up on my offer to watch Mr. Big for a couple of hours so that she could pack without having to deal with doggy bids for attention.

No kitty bid for attention greeted us as Laddie, Mr. Big, and I went home and entered the kitchen. Instead, Mona Lisa leaped to the top of her kitty tree and regarded me with disdain. The dogs paid no attention. Despite having had plenty of playtime while they were together at Belle's, both canines were peppy, so I took them out to the backyard for a romp, which didn't dissipate their energy in the slightest, so I decided to take them for a walk. The minute I reached for their leashes, they ran to me. Mr. Big wiggled as I snapped his leash on his collar, and Laddie pranced with anticipation. I grabbed my cell phone and keys, and we were out the door and on our way to the park. I wound both leashes around my wrist before I called Rebecca and told her we were headed her way. She said she'd meet me at the park.

"Where are Skippy and Tucker?" I asked when she showed up alone.

"Taking a nap, and so is Greg. I didn't want to wake them up."

"How is Greg?"

"Still acting kind of weird. I brought the subject of his strange behavior up to him again, but he refused to admit that anything's wrong, so I dropped it. If he won't tell me what's bothering him, I can't force it."

"Well, maybe he'll come around soon."

"I certainly hope so. By the way, I told Josh that you found the painting I'd mentioned to him and, now that it's clear that someone stole it from the house, he was very concerned. He's going to report it to the police."

"That's good." I had to admit I was glad Josh was taking the case of the missing painting seriously now that it had mysteriously turned up at an auctioneer's shop in Scottsdale. I wouldn't have to contact Lieutenant Belmont, after all, a fact that didn't displease me, since the grumpy lieutenant always managed to get under my skin with his abrasive manner. I'd hoped his brush with death a few months earlier would have made some impact on him and his gruff manner, but no such luck.

Rebecca walked around the park with us. She said she'd keep me posted about the painting, although neither of us thought it likely that we'd learn much until after the holidays.

On the way home from the park, Laddie and Mr. Big began showing signs of finally tiring, and, when we arrived, they both flopped down on the floor in the living room and fell fast asleep while I went to the studio to make sure everything was in order for the evening's tour. Laddie and Mr. Big didn't wake up until Emma came home, with Dennis right behind her.

"Belle called to ask me to pick up Mr. Big," he explained.

The little white dog ran in circles around Dennis's legs until Dennis scooped him up and held him in his arms.

"I guess I'll be carrying him home," Dennis said with a grin, as I handed him Mr. Big's leash. "We'll drop him off in the morning. See you then."

"I forgot to check with Belle. What time?"

"Better make it seven. That'll give us plenty of time to drive to the airport and find a long-term parking spot."

"All right. Sounds good. We'll be waiting for him."

Laddie might have been sad at his little buddy's departure, but his thoughts had clearly turned to dinner. As soon as I fed him and Mona Lisa, I realized there wasn't much time before tour hours started.

"I'm going to put the sign out and turn on the Christmas lights," I told Emma. "We can go ahead and have dinner—I'm warming up a casserole—but I'll need to keep an eye out for customers."

"No problem. Why don't I make a salad?"

"Good. I'll be back in a minute."

After I wheeled my sign out to the curb and checked to make sure all the Christmas lights were working, I came back into the studio and put the baby gate up in the doorway between the studio and my living room.

Emma and I were able to enjoy a leisurely dinner since not a single visitor showed up in the first half hour. We made quick work of clearing the table and putting our few dishes into the dishwasher before Emma told me that one of her friends had posted some make-up tutorials online and she wanted to watch them.

"But don't worry, Mom. You won't hear a thing. I'll use my earbuds."

After waiting for visitors for about an hour, without any arrivals, my concern about noise coming from my living room and disturbing potential customers seemed to have been unwarranted.

I went into the studio, anyway, to wait, and sat at my desk, where I powered up my laptop. Maybe I could find Eric's painting in one of the auction house's catalogs. Unfortunately, the featured photo of "Desert at Dawn" didn't link to its place in any of the catalogs.

I downloaded the first catalog and looked all the way through it, but the painting wasn't there. In the second catalog, a tagline on the first page stated that this particular auction featured "major mid-century works." As I viewed the listings, I could see that, based on the expected prices of the artworks, the tagline was accurate. I began scrolling through the listings, and it wasn't long before I found "Desert at Dawn."

I almost fell off my chair when I read the auction estimate of five to ten million dollars. Eric's painting was worth a fortune!

Chapter 40

Immediately, it dawned on me that the object Eric had wanted to show Susan must have been the painting and not his copy of the lawsuit against the helicopter company.

At the same time, I realized who had poisoned the carrot bars at the fair and killed Eric. It occurred to me that he had been the target all along and that the other poisoning victims were collateral damage, people a ruthless killer had used in a scheme to confuse the police.

I called the station right away and asked for Lieutenant Belmont. I wasn't too surprised when the duty officer told me he wasn't in, but I begged him to convey a message that it was urgent that I speak to the lieutenant. He hesitated, so I asked for the chief. Of course, he wasn't there, either, but, finally, the officer agreed to call Lieutenant Belmont and give him my message.

I was pacing back and forth while waiting for him to call when the first customers of the evening, a family of four with two teenagers, arrived. Although it was difficult to switch gears, I forced myself to concentrate on them and answer their questions. The girls seemed especially interested in my paintings.

"We're taking art this year," one of them volunteered. "I wish I could paint as well as you do," she said, studying my portraits of Laddie and Mona Lisa.

"You'll get there," I assured her. "It takes a lot of practice and time to develop your own style."

After they browsed for some time, the parents told their daughters they could each pick out one print as an early Christmas present. The teenagers took their time going through the boxes of prints I had available. The girl who'd spoken to me earlier selected a cute portrait of two pugs, and her sister picked out a landscape. Their father paid with cash, a rare occurrence. Most people charged their purchases.

We all wished each other a Merry Christmas as they left the studio.

I checked the time and realized it had been forty-five minutes since I'd talked to the police officer on duty, and Lieutenant Belmont still hadn't returned my call. I called the station again and learned that the officer hadn't been able to contact Lieutenant Belmont, although he promised he'd keep trying. Frustrated, I thanked him for continuing to try, emphasizing how important it was that I speak to the lieutenant.

After I disconnected, I called Dawn, knowing Dave would understand the significance of my information, but my call went to her voicemail. I left a message before searching the Roadrunner's directory of members. Some members had listed both landlines and their mobile phone numbers. I confirmed that both Dawn and her mother Dorothy had home phones, and I felt sure I'd be able to reach Dave as I called Dawn's house phone. Nobody answered, so I left an urgent message before taking my last shot by calling Dorothy. Perhaps Dawn and Dave were at her house right now. If not, she might know where they were. Not only didn't Dorothy pick up, but she obviously didn't have a message machine, either, because the phone just kept ringing and I was never prompted to leave a message.

Reluctantly, I realized I'd have to wait for a call back.

Studio tour hours would end in a few minutes. I went to the door leading to the living room to tell Emma I was about to shut it down for the night. She was looking at her laptop while Laddie lay at her feet and Mona Lisa slept on her perch atop her kitty tree.

Glued to her laptop screen and wearing earbuds, Emma didn't notice me, but Laddie jumped up. Just as he ran to the baby gate and I reached out to pet him, I heard the studio door open.

I whirled around, and my heart sank when I saw who it was.

Chapter 41

Struggling to maintain my composure, I greeted my visitor. He looked like a lumberjack in a quilted, red-and-black buffalo plaid shirt jacket, jeans, and work boots. That he carried an aluminum baking tray seemed incongruous, to say the least.

Laddie began wagging his tail in anticipation of meeting a new friend.

"He looks like a golden retriever."

"That's right."

"What's his name?"

"Laddie."

"Well, I bet Laddie would like a treat, wouldn't you, boy?"

At the mention of a "treat," Laddie began panting and whipping his tail back and forth even faster.

My visitor approached him, removed the aluminum foil from the top of the crinkled tray he carried, and took out a brownie, which he offered Laddie.

"No!" I yelled, startling him so much that he dropped the brownie. "Chocolate can poison dogs. It can be toxic if they eat it," I said, as I grabbed some paper towels from my supply table, picked up the offending snack from the floor, discarded it in the trash can, and wiped the floor clean.

Downcast, Laddie watched in disappointment as I got rid of the brownie.

"Really? I didn't know that. Chocolate's not poisonous to people, though. I brought you these as a thank-you for letting Rebecca know you found Eric's picture." Josh set the tray down on top of my desk.

"Oh, OK, thanks," I said hesitantly. "I was just about to close for the evening. If you don't mind . . . ."

I tried to sound matter-of-fact, even nonchalant, but I didn't succeed in pulling it off. Josh studied me closely, and, from the expression on his face, I knew he could tell I suspected him of killing his uncle.

"I'm afraid I do mind," he said, and there was no mistaking the menace in his voice.

I wanted to call out to Emma to warn her, but she hadn't appeared at the door when I'd raised my voice to stop Josh from feeding Laddie a brownie, so I knew she was still watching videos and couldn't hear me.

"I need to buy a Christmas present for Kayla," he said abruptly, grabbing the first print in the box closest to him. Without bothering to glance at it, he tossed the picture, a colorful abstract landscape, on my desk, along with his credit card, and waited while I processed the sale. I didn't know how far he intended to take the charade, but I played along with him, although I couldn't keep my hands from shaking as I slipped the print into a bag. He headed for the outside door, and I was hoping against hope that he'd leave, but he set the print next to the door and came back toward me.

He picked up the tray of brownies and held it out to me. "Have one." It sounded more like a command than an invitation.

"I don't think so."

"I *said* have one!" he snarled. He'd dropped all pretense now.

With only my desk between us, I looked around, trying to figure out how to escape. On the other side of the baby gate, Laddie, his tail no longer wagging, looked at us in confusion.

I didn't want Josh to realize Emma was in the other room, and I didn't want him to hurt Laddie, either. Josh watched me as I looked at my golden boy, but I took him by surprise when I ran toward the outside door.

He was quicker than I was, and he blocked my path. "Eat one, or I'm going to give them all to your dog."

"No, please," I begged. "He hasn't done anything to hurt you."

"We can't say the same for you, can we?"

"I haven't done anything to hurt you, either. You're the one who's hurting people."

Josh shrugged. "They were in the wrong place at the wrong time."

"And your uncle? What did he ever do to you?"

"I liked Uncle Eric. He was a good guy. Too bad he had to go, but he probably would have lived another thirty, maybe forty, years. Too long to wait for my inheritance."

"I bet you went to Brooks Miller's gallery with him when he decided to find out if his wife's old painting was worth anything," I said. "That's how you found out about it."

I was desperately trying to stall Josh, but I could tell what little patience he had was wearing thin.

He took a step toward me.

I backed up. "Wait!" I cried. "Where did you get the hemlock?"

"What difference does it make?"

"Just curious."

225

"Curiosity killed the cat. If you weren't so nosy, you wouldn't be in trouble right now. If you must know, I harvested it next to the creek up at the Equine Center. That old busybody next door to Uncle Eric's took our science class there on a field trip. She showed us exactly what it looks like. Only time in her life she was ever actually helpful."

He took another few steps toward me, and I backed up until there was no place to go. He grabbed me, picked up a brownie, and tried to force it into my mouth, but I refused to part my lips.

Just as I drew my arm across my face to wipe the brownie off that he'd smeared on it, Emma appeared behind Laddie.

"Mom! What's going on?"

"Run!" I screamed.

"Stay right where you are!" Josh commanded her.

Emma hesitated.

He pushed me in front of him and put his left arm around my neck, before withdrawing something from his pocket.

I felt the pinch of a blade on my neck. A knife!

Then, I realized he held a box cutter. Although the instrument was small, it could be as deadly as a knife.

Holding it to my throat, he nudged me toward the baby gate.

Laddie yelped, and Emma patted her leg, urging him to come to her.

Without loosening his grip on me, Josh kicked the baby gate, and it fell, clattering to the floor.

Laddie growled. I'd never heard him do that before; the friendliest of dogs, my golden boy had a sweet disposition, but he'd picked up on Josh's bad vibes. Abruptly, his growling ended with a sharp bark.

"Keep that dog away from me," Josh told Emma. "Sit down!"

She backed up, sank to the sofa, and coaxed Laddie to stay by her side. "You're going to kill us, aren't you?" Emma sobbed, putting her arm around Laddie, who began to whine.

"Of course not," Josh declared. "I just want to talk some sense into your mother."

"I don't believe you," she said.

"Suit yourself," he told Emma. Whispering to me, "wrong place at the wrong time," he pricked my neck again.

My blood boiled. He regarded my daughter as nothing more than collateral damage, the same way he'd thought of the innocent people he'd poisoned at the high school and the same way he thought of me, too, for that matter.

For once in my life, I wished I were wearing the highest, spikiest heels available so that I could stomp on his instep. The flats I was wearing had hard soles, but they wouldn't have the same effect. Still, I had to try.

Holding my foot at an angle to catch his instep with the edge of the heel, I brought it down as hard as I could.

"Ow!" Distracted for the moment, Josh loosened his grip, hopping on one foot.

Mona Lisa, who'd hadn't come down from her perch all evening, launched herself at Josh, landing on his head, and raked her sharp front claws across his face. He yowled like a banshee, as he put both hands up to get to her, but she was too quick, and she jumped down, out of his way. Rushing forward, Laddie chomped on Josh's right wrist, and the killer dropped the box cutter.

It skittered across the floor, toward Emma; she kicked it under the sofa.

Josh howled in pain, swinging his arm toward Laddie, who

was behind him now, nipping at his legs.

He reached out to grab me again, but missed. I came back, butting my head into his stomach; losing his balance, he fell.

Emma grabbed a book from the coffee table and hit him with it, but it wasn't a heavy volume, and the blows didn't seem to phase him.

Desperately, I looked around for something I could use as a weapon. Emma's laptop! Snatching it, I brought it down on Josh's head, but he rolled to the side at the last second, and the blow glanced off him.

In the midst of our struggle, I heard the studio door open.

"Amanda, you forgot to bring your sign in," Dennis called.

"Help!" I yelled.

He joined us in a flash, and, with all of us struggling and Laddie continuing to nip Josh's legs, we finally subdued him.

As Emma, Dennis, and I sat on top of him, Dennis asked, "Do you still have the roll of electrical tape I gave you?"

"In the kitchen. I'll get it."

As soon as I got up, Josh started scuffling again, while Dennis, Emma, and Laddie fought to control him.

I returned in a few seconds, pulling at the end of the tape, as Dennis yanked Josh's hands together behind his back and began winding the tape around his wrists. After he secured Josh's wrists, he bound his ankles together and then stood up, panting.

Josh wasn't going anywhere now.

For the final blow, Mona Lisa crept out, from under my arm chair, pounced on Josh's head again, and scratched his neck.

"Get that cat off me!" Josh yelled, but she'd already departed, this time to her perch atop her kitty tree.

Emma and I hugged each other for dear life, while Dennis

announced, "I'm calling the cops," as he pulled his cell phone from his pocket.

"Who *is* this guy, Mom?" Emma asked, as we waited for the police to arrive. "Why did he attack you?"

"It's a long story, sweetheart. I'll tell you all about it as soon as—"

"Yeah, tell *me* all about it," Lieutenant Belmont said.

I hadn't even heard him come in. The two patrol officers behind him hauled Josh up, off the floor.

"Looks like he fought it out with a wild cat."

"Meow!" Mona Lisa stood up on her perch, stretched, and turned her back on us.

For the first time, Lieutenant Belmont noticed Mona Lisa, and he actually smiled. "Your wild cat, I presume."

Chapter 42

Thankfully, events took a turn for the better after our harrowing evening. When the patrol officers left with Josh in handcuffs and the brownies he'd brought in an evidence bag, I told Lieutenant Belmont the gist of the story while Laddie hung out at his side. The last time Laddie had seen the lieutenant, paramedics had been wheeling him out of my house on a gurney after he'd suffered a heart attack.

"We have enough to go on for now," he told us. "You can all come down to the station and give your formal statements tomorrow, and don't worry. With all the charges he's facing, young Mr. Thompson won't be bailing out of jail."

"I'm going out of town tomorrow, Bill," Dennis said. As soon as he called the lieutenant "Bill," I remembered that the two knew each other. They had been at odds in the past, and Dennis didn't think much of him.

"Christmas vacation?"

"Going to visit the kids and the grandkids in Michigan."

"We can take your statement when you get back. You might want to jot down a few notes, so you can remember exactly what happened."

"I'm not likely to forget." For a second, I thought that their dislike for each other might surface, but Dennis continued, "I'll be sure to do that, though."

After Lieutenant Belmont left and we told an incredulous Belle, who'd come over as soon as she'd heard the police sirens, about my unexpected visitor, I urged my friends to go home and get some sleep since they needed to get up early to catch their flight.

Shortly after Belle and Dennis went home, Emma, Mona Lisa, Laddie, and I piled onto the sofa for a group snuggle. Emma and I stayed up half the night, talking, with a break for cocoa and cookies. We had to reward our attack pets, too, so I gave Laddie a sugar cookie and Mona Lisa one of the tuna treats she loved so much.

We slept only a few hours before Belle and Dennis dropped off Mr. Big early the next morning. We were tired but much more relaxed and grateful that life was getting back to normal.

It certainly felt that way on Christmas Day, as my family enjoyed our Christmas dinner. We moved the card table I'd borrowed from Belle and Dennis up against my tiny table so that we could all sit down together. Although the house seemed even smaller with five adults, two dogs, and one kitty, all in the same space, it also felt cozy and comfortable.

Since my family had arrived, we'd gone to a holiday concert given by the Pioneers at a local theater, followed by a tour of Lonesome Valley to see all the lights. On Christmas Eve, we'd visited a living nativity scene featuring a cooperative camel and attended church services later that evening. Focusing on the familiar traditions shared with my children and parents felt good, especially after the miserable Christmas we'd had the year before.

Not only my spirits, but my checkbook also got a bounce

while Dustin and my parents were visiting. The day after Christmas, I found I had even more reason to celebrate when Ian Adams called me with good news: He'd sold the painting that Melinda had bought but ultimately rejected. Needless to say, I was absolutely thrilled to learn of my first sale at a Scottsdale gallery. Since Emma's laptop hadn't survived my attempt to bash Josh over the head, the painting's sale gave me the perfect opportunity to replace it without going into debt, too.

A few days later, after my parents returned to Florida and Dustin to Kansas City, I headed to the Roadrunner to work the final half-day stint of my schedule for December. Emma had the afternoon off from her job at the feed store, and she was keeping an eye on Mr. Big and Laddie. During the entire time my family had been visiting, we hadn't dared leave them at home without supervision, so a friendly neighborhood dog sitter had watched them a few times. There had been an unfortunate incident with a shredded pillow at Belle's once, and I'd learned my lesson. Fortunately, the dogs hadn't tired of each other's company, but I knew Mr. Big missed Belle and Dennis. They were due home from their trip in the evening, so the little guy wouldn't have long to wait.

I arrived at the gallery the same time Susan did, and Chip was getting ready to head out. Although I'd spoken to Susan and told her all the details of Josh's attack on Emma and me, I hadn't talked to Chip since Josh had come calling at my studio.

"Amanda!" He rushed to give me a big hug. Stepping back, he said, "I'm so sorry! Josh and I have been friends since grade school. It's still hard for me to believe he poisoned his uncle."

"I'm afraid he's a sociopath, Chip, but he hid it well—most of the time, anyway."

"Kayla and I have been talking, and we came to the same conclusion. There were a few signs along the way; I see that now, but it wasn't obvious at the time."

"How's Kayla doing?"

"She's devastated, of course. Josh sent word through his lawyer that he wanted to talk to her, but she refused. She doesn't want anything to do with him."

"A wise decision on her part," Susan said. "Josh always seemed like such a nice, polite boy whenever I saw him." She shook her head. "I still can't believe it."

"Well, I'd better get going. Valerie just left a minute ago, so it's up to you two to hold down the fort. She told me the Roadrunner was swamped the day after Christmas, but it's been pretty quiet since then."

Chip was right. There wasn't a single customer in the gallery.

"There's one thing I don't understand," Susan said, after Chip left. "Remember you told me Josh bought a print from you?"

"Uh, huh. Of course, it was still there when the police arrested him, so I put it back in stock and issued a refund to his credit card."

"Why do you think he bought it?"

"I'm not really sure, but my best guess is that he thought he could cover his tracks. His fingerprints were on the door, and he touched some other things when he was in the studio. With my print and receipt, he could have explained why he was there. Of course, he would have had to get rid of that tray of brownies."

"Makes sense. I feel bad for Kayla. Remember how she blamed herself for bringing Eric the carrot bars?"

"Yes, I'll bet Josh steered her right to them, but in a way that made her think it was her own idea."

"That could be. By the way, I bumped into Gina yesterday at the supermarket, and she's disgusted with Kevin, even though she bailed him out so that he wouldn't have to spend Christmas in jail. She said he became so obsessed with getting back the money Eric owed him that he kind of went off the deep end."

"I'll say. Speaking of Kevin, that reminds me. I wonder what happened to Natalie's costume jewelry. Kevin obviously didn't steal it. The only pieces of jewelry the police found on him after he broke into Eric's house were the pearl necklace and diamond ring."

"Eric donated all Natalie's costume jewelry to the charity shop. I went over to the house a few months after Natalie died to help him clear out her things, but we got only as far as the costume jewelry before he broke down and couldn't bring himself to donate her clothes. He asked me to drop off the bag of jewelry at the charity shop. Naturally, I did. I knew he could never force himself to do it."

"Well, that solves one mystery. Eric's neighbor, Sylvia Costa, was wearing a large poinsettia brooch the day Kevin broke into the house. Rebecca thought it had belonged to Natalie. She thought Sylvia might have gone into the house and taken it, but she must have bought it at the charity shop."

The next day, another mystery was solved when Rebecca called me to tell me she finally found out why Greg had been acting so strangely. He'd been having chest pains and was so petrified by his possible imminent demise that he hadn't gone to the emergency room or even called his doctor until he felt worse and told Rebecca.

"He spent all day yesterday having tests," Rebecca told me, "and now his doctor's diagnosed him with angina pectoris. One thing the doctor told him is that stress aggravates his condition, and he's certainly had a lot of that lately, what with Eric's death and finding out Josh killed him. Thank goodness, the doc says Greg will be fine. He needs to take some medication when he has pain, but he should be OK."

"That's a relief."

"For both of us. I wish he'd said something sooner, but at least we found out what's wrong. He wasn't feeling at all well on Christmas Day when we were visiting the kids in Houston, but I expect New Year's will be a different story. By the way, I hear you're having a project for the new year."

"You mean the garage?"

"Yes. I ran into Belle and Dennis at the park a little while ago, and they told me all about it."

"It's great, isn't it? It will be so nice to have a real garage. I'll have an automatic garage door, too."

Thanks to Dennis, I thought. After he'd found out that the city building permit for my garage project had never been issued, he'd gone to Lonesome Valley City Hall himself and learned that the delay was due to the mayor. Miraculously, when he mentioned he knew a few members of the city council, the permit was issued. He and Brian planned to start and, hopefully, finish, construction the day after New Year's.

Brian had made reservations for us to dine at one of the Resort's swankiest restaurants on New Year's Eve. He arrived home a few hours before he was due to pick me up and called to let me know he'd finally made it back to Lonesome Valley after waiting for a delayed flight to take off, but I wouldn't see him until our dinner date.

Emma had a date of her own for New Year's Eve. Dennis's suspicion that she liked a certain young man who worked at the feed store had been spot on. Matt was an Air Force veteran, six years older than Emma, and he was going to college part-time while acting as assistant manager at the feed store. I met him briefly when he picked Emma up, and I was impressed with his manner. From the way Emma looked at him, I knew she was, too.

I'd decided to go all out for my date with Brian. I had my hair and nails done at a salon and bought a sparkly new purple dress and high heels for the occasion. As I put on my false eyelashes, I wondered if maybe I was taking it a bit too far. I normally didn't wear so much make-up, but when Brian came to pick me up, I knew it had been worth it.

"Wow!" he said, scooping me up in his arms. "You look fantastic! Ready to celebrate New Year's?"

"I certainly am! I'm looking forward to a great New Year."

"Me, too," he said.

Although Mona Lisa, surveying us from atop her kitty tree's perch, seemed indifferent, Laddie barked approvingly, as Brian kissed me.

Have you read all the books in the Fine Art Mystery Series? If so, you will also enjoy Paula Darnell's cozy mystery DIY Diva Series.

Recipes

Bourbon Balls

These holiday goodies taste better when allowed to "ripen" overnight so that the bourbon flavor can permeate the cookie. They make a nice little Christmas gift when packaged in a decorative, airtight tin. As their name implies, these ball-shaped cookies contain real bourbon whiskey, so they're not for teetotalers. Use a high-quality bourbon for the best results. Added bonus: no baking is required!

Ingredients for Cookies

1 eleven-ounce box of vanilla wafers
1 ¼ cup finely chopped pecans
2 tablespoons cocoa
2 tablespoons dark corn syrup
1/3 cup bourbon whiskey

Ingredients for Rolling Cookies

4 tablespoons cocoa
1 ½ cup powdered sugar

Directions

Pulverize the vanilla wafers in a food processor, or put them in a gallon freezer bag, zip it closed, and crush them with a rolling pin. Chop the pecans into very small pieces. Put the dry ingredients into a mixing bowl and slowly add the dark corn syrup and the bourbon. Mix the ingredients well until the dough holds together when formed into small balls. Set the cookie mixture aside and combine the cocoa and powdered sugar for rolling the cookies. Mix well. Form the dough into balls about 1 to 1 ¼ inch in diameter. Dust your hands (or your gloved hands) with powdered sugar, and roll each ball in the cocoa-powdered sugar mixture until it's completely covered. Store in an airtight container. Let the bourbon balls sit to "ripen" for at least 24 hours before serving them.

Makes about four dozen bourbon balls.

Chocolate-Dipped Butterscotch Shortbread Cookies

This recipe was contributed by Andrea Wilder. These yummy, rich cookies are a perfect accompaniment to coffee or tea, and they make an excellent treat for the holidays.

Ingredients

1 cup butter
¾ cup brown sugar
1 teaspoon vanilla
2 cups flour
1 teaspoon salt
¾ cup butterscotch chips
8 ounces dark chocolate

Directions

Soften the butter before beginning. Preheat the oven to 300 degrees. Beat the butter and brown sugar until the mixture is light and fluffy. Add the vanilla and mix. Slowly add the flour and salt until just combined. Add the butterscotch chips and mix slowly until evenly distributed. Grease an eight-inch by eight-inch baking pan. Using a rubber spatula, press the dough evenly into the pan. Refrigerate the dough for twenty minutes. Remove the dough from the refrigerator and score it into sixteen squares. Pierce the dough all over with a fork. Bake about an hour until firm and golden brown around the edges. Remove from the oven and immediately cut through the scoring marks to separate the cookies. Move the pan to a wire rack and cool completely.

Chop the dark chocolate and place it in a microwave-safe bowl. Microwave in twenty-second intervals, stirring each time, until the chocolate is melted. Remove cookies from the baking pan and place them on a cookie sheet lined with parchment paper. Dip each shortbread cookie into the chocolate mixture and return to the cookie sheet. Refrigerate the cookies for approximately thirty minutes, until the chocolate is set. Store the cookies in an airtight container in the refrigerator for up to three weeks. Remove cookies from the refrigerator twenty to thirty minutes before serving.

Makes sixteen shortbread cookies.

Chocolate Stove-top Oatmeal Cookies

This recipe was contributed by Katherine Black. According to Kathy, it's been around for a long time. She first made cookies from this recipe over sixty years ago. She suggests that you measure the oats and peanut butter before beginning and put the vanilla nearby because things will happen quickly once the mixture begins to boil.

Ingredients

2 cups sugar
½ cup cocoa
½ cup milk
½ cup butter
3 cups quick-cooking oats
½ cup creamy peanut butter
1 teaspoon vanilla

Directions

Lay out parchment paper on the counter near the stove. Measure oats, peanut butter, and vanilla and have them standing by. Put the sugar, cocoa, and milk into a saucepan on a stove burner. Turn on the burner to medium. Add the butter and bring the mixture to a boil, stirring constantly. Stop stirring when the mixture begins to boil and continue boiling for one minute.* Remove the mixture immediately and quickly add the oats, peanut butter, and vanilla. Stir to blend the ingredients. Drop and shape by the large spoonful onto the parchment paper. Let the cookies set until cool. Store the cookies in an airtight container.

Makes about two dozen cookies.

*According to Kathy, the boiling time can be a bit tricky, so she uses a candy thermometer to test whether the mixture is ready. The candy thermometer should register the soft ball stage (235 to 240 degrees). Another method to determine whether the mixture is ready is to scoop some up in a spoon, tip it, and watch how it drops. If it is dropping very slowly, the mixture is ready.

Holiday Meringue Cookies

This recipe was contributed by Andrea Wilder. Crushed peppermint gives these delicate cookies a bit of a holiday vibe because red-and-white-striped peppermint candy canes are so closely associated with Christmas, but, according to Andrea, you can omit the peppermint in this recipe, if you prefer.

Ingredients

2 egg whites
1/8 teaspoon salt
1/8 teaspoon cream of tartar
¾ cup fine sugar
½ teaspoon vanilla
1 cup semisweet chocolate chips
3 tablespoons crushed peppermint candies

Directions

Make sure the egg whites are at room temperature before beginning. Preheat the oven to 250 degrees. Beat the egg whites with an electric mixer until they are foamy. Add the salt and cream of tartar. Continue beating the mixture until soft peaks form. Add the sugar, one tablespoon at a time, and beat well after each addition. Continue beating until the mixture is stiff. With a spatula, fold in the vanilla, chocolate chips, and crushed peppermint by hand.

Line a baking sheet with parchment paper. Drop the mixture

by teaspoonfuls, one-half inch apart, on a greased baking sheet. Bake for forty minutes. Cool and store in an airtight container.

Makes about four dozen cookies.

Pinwheel Cookies

Pinwheel cookies owe their name to their spiral shape. Traditionally, they are made with one vanilla layer and one chocolate layer. For a holiday version, simply add a few drops of red food coloring in the vanilla layer and substitute green food coloring for chocolate in the second layer, and when you roll them up, they'll look like red and green spirals.

Ingredients

1 1/3 cups sugar
1 cup butter
1 teaspoon vanilla
2 large eggs
½ teaspoon baking powder
¼ teaspoon salt
3 cups flour
2 ounces (squares) unsweetened baking chocolate

Directions

Soften the butter and melt the chocolate before beginning. Cream the softened butter with the sugar. Add the eggs and vanilla and beat. Mix the baking powder, salt, and flour in a separate bowl and slowly add to the first mixture. Divide the dough in half, and put one half on a sheet of parchment paper and shape it into a rectangle. In the mixing bowl, add the melted chocolate to the other half of the dough and mix well. Turn out onto a sheet of parchment paper and shape it into a rectangle the same size as the vanilla dough. Cover each rectangle with parchment paper, and put them into the refrigerator to chill for at least half an hour.

Remove dough from the refrigerator and roll each half of the dough, maintaining a rectangle shape, into a layer about 12 inches by 16 inches (trim dough to even the edges) and about 1/8 inch thick. Carefully, place the chocolate layer on top of the vanilla layer. Cover the dough with parchment paper and refrigerate it for at least half an hour. From the sixteen-inch side, roll the dough into a log, keeping it tight. Wrap the dough log in plastic wrap. Refrigerate the dough for at least three hours or overnight.

Preheat the oven to 350 degrees. Slice the dough into ¼-inch-thick slices and place each cookie on a parchment-lined baking sheet. Bake about 8 to 10 minutes. When the vanilla layer is slightly golden and the cookies are "set," remove the cookies, and cool them on a wire rack.

Makes about four dozen cookies.

Sugar Cookies

This recipe was contributed by Katherine Black, who originally received it from Alton Brown. Kathy says that Alton is "as ever, the best chef." For the holidays, use cookie cutters with shapes such as a Christmas tree, snowman, or candy cane. Note that you will be using confectioners powdered sugar when you roll out the cookies. According to Kathy, it works very well and actually sweetens the cookies, too.

Ingredients for Cookies

3 cups flour
¾ teaspoon baking powder
¼ teaspoon salt
1 cup unsalted butter
1 cup sugar
1 egg
1 tablespoon milk
confectioners powdered sugar for rolling out the dough

Ingredients for Icing

½ cup butter
1 one-pound package confectioners powdered sugar
2 tablespoons milk
food coloring (select colors based on which shapes you're making)

Directions

Soften the butter and beat the egg before beginning. Sift the flour, baking powder, and salt together and set aside. Place the butter and sugar in a large bowl of an electric stand mixer and beat until light in color. Add beaten egg and milk and beat to combine. Set the mixer on low speed and gradually add the flour mixture. Beat until the dough pulls away from the sides of the bowl. Divide the dough in half, wrap it in parchment paper, and refrigerate it for two hours. Put a cookie sheet in the freezer to chill.

Preheat the oven to 375 degrees. Using a sifter, sprinkle one tablespoon of confectioners powdered sugar on the rolling surface. Remove dough from the refrigerator, one package at a time. Sprinkle a rolling pin with confectioners powdered sugar. Roll out the dough to an even thickness of ¼ inch. If the dough becomes too warm, place the chilled cookie sheet in the freezer on top of the dough for ten minutes. Cut the rolled dough into shapes with cookie cutters and place the cookies at least one inch apart on cookie sheets lined with parchment paper.

Bake eight to twelve minutes, rotating the cookie sheet once after about four or five minutes. Remove the cookies from the oven when they are just beginning to turn brown on the edges. Let the cookies cool for two minutes on the cookie sheet before moving them to a wire rack to finish cooling them. The cookies should be completely cool before they are iced.

To make the icing, combine one package of confectioners powdered sugar with ½ cup butter. Slowly add the milk and mix in until the icing is the desired consistency. Separate the icing into small bowls, one each for each color you will be using. Add food coloring to each bowl, one drop at a time, until the icing is the desired color. Ice the cookies, and add sprinkles, if desired. Store the cookies in an airtight container.

Makes about three dozen cookies.

ABOUT THE AUTHOR

Award-winning author Paula Darnell is a former college instructor who has a Bachelor of Arts degree in English from the University of Iowa and a Master of Arts degree in English with a Writing Emphasis from the University of Nevada, Reno. *Hemlock for the Holidays* is the third book in her Fine Art Mystery series. She's also the author of the DIY Diva Mystery series and *The Six-Week Solution*, a historical mystery set in Nevada. She resides in Las Vegas with her husband Gary.

VISIT HER WEBSITE
pauladarnellauthor.com

Have you read all the books in the Fine Art Mystery series? If so, you will also enjoy Paula Darnell's cozy mystery DIY Diva series.

Made in the USA
Las Vegas, NV
24 January 2022

42227484R00152